FERALLY FUNNY FREAKSHOW

AN AC SILLY CIRCUS CO. MYSTERY

WRITTEN BY
ANN CHARLES

ILLUSTRATIONS BY
C. S. KUNKLE

To Clint the Clown.
You keep me smiling!

Also by Ann Charles

Deadwood Mystery Series

Nearly Departed in Deadwood (Book 1)
Optical Delusions in Deadwood (Book 2)
Dead Case in Deadwood (Book 3)
Better Off Dead in Deadwood (Book 4)
An Ex to Grind in Deadwood (Book 5)
Meanwhile, Back in Deadwood (Book 6)
Wild Fright in Deadwood (Book 7)
Rattling the Heat in Deadwood (Book 8)
Gone Haunting in Deadwood (Book 9)
Don't Let it Snow in Deadwood (Book 10)

Deadwood Shorts: Seeing Trouble (Book 1.5)
Deadwood Shorts: Boot Points (Book 4.5)
Deadwood Shorts: Cold Flame (Book 6.5)
Deadwood Shorts: Tequila & Time (Book 8.5)

Jackrabbit Junction Mystery Series

Dance of the Winnebagos (Book 1)
Jackrabbit Junction Jitters (Book 2)
The Great Jackalope Stampede (Book 3)
The Rowdy Coyote Rumble (Book 4)
Jackrabbit Junction Short: The Wild Turkey Tango (Book 4.5)

Dig Site Mystery Series

Look What the Wind Blew In (Book 1)
Make No Bones About It (Book 2)

Goldwash Mystery Series (a future series)

The Old Man's Back in Town (Short Story)

Coming Next from Ann Charles

AC Silly Circus Co. Mystery Series

A Bunch of Monkey Malarkey (Book 2)

Acknowledgments

Thank you to Robyn Peterman for asking me to play in your sandbox. You motivated me to start this fun series.

Thank you to my husband for helping me brainstorm in this crazy new world.

Thanks to my two kids who had fun daydreaming along with me about were-characters.

Many thanks to my editing crew—first draft folks and beta readers. I appreciate you helping on such short notice.

Thank you to my brother, CS Kunkle, for sharing your freaky ideas and great cover art.

Thank you to all of my readers for coming along to enjoy the ride in this new world.

And thank you to Clint, my brother, for being such a clown growing up. You're immortalized now. Sorry I had to kill you first though.

Chapter One

Tinkerville, Mississippi

My life was one, big, fun freakshow until someone killed my favorite clown. Now, not even watching a grizzly bear eat a flaming torch made me crack a smile.

"Okay, Eugene," I said to the big bear of a man across the crystal ball from me. "What would you like to know?"

His thick brown eyebrows pinched together over the bridge of his long nose. "I have a really bad feeling about tonight's show."

My hands hovered over the ball in a holding pattern. "That's not really a question."

"I know, but I have this burning sensation in my chest about it." He pounded his barrel-like torso, thumping hard enough to make me wince.

"That's probably indigestion from those six chili dogs I saw you eating at lunch. You know those crazy monkey brothers brag about using real diced habaneros in their chili, right?" Eugene's esophagus had to be lined with glowing embers after all that heat.

"I'm telling you, it's not the chili dogs." He burped, grimacing as he held his stomach. "Well, not only the chili dogs."

As bear shapeshifters went, Eugene was the largest I'd ever seen. His freakshow act had two parts. He started out as "The Human Giant," aka the man sitting across from me at the moment. After wowing his audience with his sheer size and physique, he shifted into a werebear, risking life and fur to swallow fiery torches whole.

The act was always a crowd pleaser, reeling in folks night after night. After seeing it, nobody would ever suspect that due to an incident months ago involving a candle, an erotic romance novel, and some singed chest hair, Eugene now suffered from pyrophobia.

"I'm telling you, Electra," he said, his baritone voice hitching. "Something bad is going to happen tonight." He chewed on his thumbnail, the hair on his knuckle a thick tuft like his eyebrows.

I slid my hands over the cool, smooth crystal ball, my fingertips sparking a blue light within the orb. "Eugene, you have had a bad feeling about your flame-eating act every day since the candle accident." His cheeks darkened, his gaze lowering to his hands. "That's why we consult Ol' Blue before each performance, remember?"

Passed down through my family line for too many generations to count, the crystal eye had been called *Chosposi* by the ancient ones, which translated into "bluebird eye." However, I preferred to use "Ol' Blue," the nickname my grandmother had given the all-seeing ball before passing it down to me after my mother opted out of using her power of sight.

Eugene sighed. "But tonight feels worse than before."

I didn't bother reminding him that he also said that every evening before his show. "Why does it feel worse?"

"Because Clint the Clown is dead."

Hmmm. That was a different reason than usual. "Honey, Clint has been gone for over a week now."

"I know, but I keep thinking about the last thing he said to me."

"What was that?"

"He wanted me to hold onto the key to his roller skates because he kept misplacing it."

I frowned. "They still use keys on those things?"

"Clint's skates were old school. They were the metal slip-on kind that expanded to fit over his clown shoes." Eugene smiled wistfully. "Good old Clint could sure put on one hell of a show on those skates."

As tragic as the death of a clown was, life had to keep rolling on for Eugene … and for me. I had shed plenty of tears over the last week. Fat, clown-sized tears. Clint had been the light that kept the rest of us tumbling along night after night. His was the last act each evening, sending the crowd to their cars with wide smiles. The world had lost some of its sparkle when Clint died.

"We have to move on," I told Eugene. "Clint would want it that way."

Actually, we had moved on—literally. We'd loaded up our circus train and chugged along the tracks to the next stop here in Tinkerville, where we were booked for a week solid.

Come one, come all to see the Feral Freakshow, our marketing department advertised, churning up crowds full of shapeshifting spectators both young and old. We had were-freaks and were-clowns aplenty to entertain the masses, along with a few plain old animals that were treated like royalty among the circus were-folks.

"I think Clint's death was a sign," Eugene said.

"What sort of sign?" To never take life for granted?

I rubbed my fingertips over the cool crystal ball, remembering the big clown smile Clint always painted on his face. The blue light inside the glass swirled like smoke, following my touch. Unlike Eugene, myself, and many others here at the circus, Clint had stayed in costume whenever leaving his tent. His rainbow hair always stuck out in a crowd, just like his upbeat personality.

Why on earth would someone want to kill a damned clown? A guy whose main goal was to make people laugh? I still couldn't wrap my mind around it.

"A sign that I'm supposed to stop eating fire," Eugene said, pulling me out of my reverie.

We'd gone over this before, only not using Clint's death as a reason. Eugene kept grasping at straws for excuses to put down his torches. Not that I could blame him. Shoving oversized lighted matchsticks down my throat didn't appeal to me either. I was glad my act involved a cushy chair, a bit of showmanship, a few tricks of the crystal ball trade, and that was it.

"That wasn't the only sign, either," he told me, his brown, teddy bear eyes round with worry.

"What other signs have you seen?"

"Someone spray painted graffiti on a bunch of our poster boards again, messing with our name."

Actually, I'd foreseen this several nights ago in Ol' Blue and warned Runash, the circus's new head of security, to keep a look out for three teenage raccoons trying to sneak into the circus with spray cans. Runash had rolled her eyes at my prediction and told me to stick to entertaining the paying customers.

Same shit, different security jerk.

"What did they paint on the poster boards this time?" I asked Eugene. I'd seen the raccoons at work in the crystal ball, but not the finished product. Ol' Blue was a tease most nights, giving me only glimpses of possible futures and murky peeks of set pasts.

"Our name. It now reads: *FeralLY Funny Freakshow.*"

Playing Polly Positive, I said, "In my line of work, I'd see that as a prophecy. Maybe it's time to mix up our acts, add humor instead of getting our freak on every night."

"What's funny about a fire eater?"

"Think outside the box, Eugene."

He scratched behind one of his small ears, his face scrunched. "Ming says she's going to write something new about Clint's death."

That blogger bitch needed to cap her damned pen before someone did it for her. "That nose of hers is going to get her into trouble some day, mark my words."

"Is that what your crystal ball says?"

"No, that's just the word from my lips to your ears."

Ming had been sniffing around again, trying to scrounge up

some juicy dirt on Clint so she could broadcast about his tragic ending to the world. She claimed it would be an epitaph, but I had a feeling it had a lot more to do with gaining her new readers and potential sponsors.

When it came to Ming, she had one goal in mind … well, two. The first being plastic surgery to fix her hairless problem when she shifted to her weredoggy self. The other was to be called up to the journalism "majors" and land a career in the big leagues, aka television. Ming told me once she'd do whatever it took to succeed. Apparently, "whatever" included having repeated office couch sex with the circus's master of ceremonies and exploiting the death of everyone's favorite clown.

Ming's selfishness was an exception among the rest of the "hybrid" shapeshifters here at the freakshow circus, who were trying to make it in a world full of purebred shifters. Shunned outside of the red and white striped tent, the circus folks had formed a tight-knit pack of their own. It had taken me several long, lonely months to overcome their distrust of my purebred pedigree and fit in amongst their ranks.

"Listen, Eugene," I started, but then paused at the sound of a footfall on the other side of the red velvet curtains that divided my reading parlor from the waiting area. "Who's there?"

Nobody answered.

Eugene looked around. "I don't hear anyone."

That's because he was a fire-eating bear who shifted into a giant with small ears and a long nose. I, on the other hand, had the hearing of a long line of werecoyotes, no matter if my fur was showing or not.

Eugene sniffed. "Hey, I know that smell, but …"

"Whoever is on the other side of the curtains, I can hear you huffing," I said. "If you're looking for the three little pigs, Eugene ate them for dinner last night."

"I'm not eating pork anymore. The doctor says too much fat in my diet could make me more flammable."

The curtains parted. "I wasn't huffing, Electra," Bruno Maska said in his low growly voice. His broad shoulders filled the entryway into my fortune-telling parlor.

My heart staggered at the sight of the ex-head of security. His dark, wavy hair was combed back and his beard trimmed short around his square jaw. Bruno was all brawn and plenty of brains, which equaled one helluva batch of trouble for me and my bag of tricks. I tried to act cool and calm, lifting my chin when I met his brown eyes. The anger smoldering in their depths sent a quiver of nervous energy zipping through my limbs. Bruno was taking no prisoners this evening, and it appeared I was standing in his way.

Breaking eye contact, I looked down at my empty crystal ball. What was Bruno doing back here? I thought he'd moved on to lead the owner's entourage of bodyguards and secret service. When he'd left a month ago, I'd not expected to see him again, offering prayers to the moon goddess that he'd be gone from my life for good. How come I hadn't seen him when I looked into Ol' Blue earlier to check for any signs of danger tonight?

"Bruno! I thought that was your scent." Eugene lumbered to his feet, his smile wide on his large, hairy head. He wrapped Bruno in a bear hug for several seconds before stepping back. "Boy howdy, am I happy to see you again. I was just telling Electra how things don't feel as safe around here ever since Clint got killed."

"Really?" Bruno stuck his hands in his jeans pockets, taking a wide stance that blocked off any chance of my slipping past him and running for my life. His gaze narrowed when it centered on my crystal ball. "Why don't they feel safe?"

"I don't know exactly," Eugene said, wringing his thick fingers together. "But my hair keeps bristling at the base of my neck for no reason."

"It's almost full moon," I reminded him.

Eugene continued without pause. "Two nights ago, I almost lit my face on fire."

I sighed. "You singed one long hair on your muzzle."

"And now my jaw clicks every time I close it."

"That's your teeth clacking together." I grabbed my velvet shroud and draped it over Ol' Blue, my skin tingling under Bruno's watchful stare. "Eugene," I said, lacing my fingers together, trying to pretend the scent of Bruno in my tent wasn't throwing me off my game. "I want you to sing 'Jingle Bells' three times tonight before you go on stage."

A wrinkle formed on Eugene's wide brow. "But it's almost Halloween, not Christmas."

"Ol' Blue did not show me anything for you to worry about tonight. After you sing the song for the third time, you'll eat the flames, wow the crowd, and walk away once more burn-free."

"Was I wearing my new gear in your crystal ball?"

Eugene had recently purchased fireman headgear, but his ears kept getting crushed inside of the helmet, so he'd had to cut holes in it. On top of that, he couldn't figure out how to maneuver a flaming torch into his gaping jaws through the face shield, which kept fogging up from his snout pushing against it.

"No, just your fireproof face balm." I gave him my best everything-will-be-okay smile. "Trust me, your fur will still be singe-free in the morning."

He scratched his big jaw, frowning, and then turned to Bruno. "You here to see the show tonight?"

Bruno shook his head. "I'm here to bring Clint's killer to justice."

"Good. If anyone can figure out who's behind this, it's you. I always said nobody can sniff out trouble better than Bruno." Eugene gave him another bear hug, only from the side this time. Something made a popping sound and Bruno grimaced. After a wave in my direction, Eugene took his worries and left my tent.

For several silent seconds, I stared at Bruno, reminding myself of the reasons I could not let him sniff out that he was my fated mate. For starters, it could be the death of him. For enders, it could be the death of me, too.

"So, you're back," I said, cutting our standoff short.

One dark eyebrow lifted. "Surprised?"

"Not really," I lied.

"Let me guess," he said with a smirk. "Your magical crystal ball showed you that I was coming." Bruno had never been a believer in my abilities. *Once a trickster, always a trickster*, he'd said to me more than once.

"You still have that chip on your shoulder, I see." Bruno didn't trust purebred shapeshifters. According to circus gossip, his father had knocked up his mother with a half-breed child and then left, never to return.

"Only when it comes to you, Electra." He glanced around my tent, his frown growing as he took in my roadrunner incense holders, decks of tarot cards, and veil-covered lamps. "Where were you the night Clint was killed?"

I scowled. "You think I'm a suspect in his murder?"

"I know you're a suspect. Answer the question."

"Fuck you." I stood, grabbing Ol' Blue, shoving it in the lock box where I stored it.

"We tried that already. It only made this thing between us worse."

By "this thing," I assumed he meant the constant underlying attraction turned frustration thanks to the mental buffer I used to disguise my natural scent from him. It was a trick I'd learned from my grandmother long ago, a way to hide in plain sight when needed. It worked for Bruno the same as any possible bounty hunters looking for my hide since I joined the Gone Were witness protection program for shifters.

Without that buffer, not only would Bruno have figured out the real reason for the tension always hovering between us, but I couldn't have kept him at bay. According to everything I'd read since first meeting the maddeningly sexy brute, short of death, there was no resisting a fated mate.

I was toast already, itching for Bruno every night since I'd met him. However, I had one hell of a reason to keep my paws off of him, and I'd managed to do just that until a month ago at his going-away party.

I'd been drinking to forget him that night, and he'd been drinking to forget all of us. Thanks to the monkey brothers' homemade *really* hard cider, we'd both ended up sloshed. When Bruno leaned in close to accuse me yet again of turning up my nose at half-breeds, I had grabbed him by the shirt and planted my lips on his to show how I felt about the exasperating half-breed in front of me. One thing led to another and before I could lasso my emotions, I was already naked inside his tent, and then he was already naked inside of me.

I'd left him passed out on his bed, tiptoeing back to my own tent before anyone found out about us. Come morning, I'd made sure I wasn't around when Bruno said his final good-byes.

His leaving for a higher rung on the career ladder had been my saving grace, even if I had ached from missing him almost every day since. But now that he was back, I'd have to resort to my old tricks—cold showers, sniffing pepper, and, as a last resort, taming-the-shrew with my own devices when the need grew too strong.

"Answer the question, Electra."

"The night Clint was killed, I was in my tent in bed."

His gaze hardened. "Alone?"

"That's none of your business."

"Alone or not?"

"Of course I was alone."

"Right, because there were no other drunk, half-breed suckers willing to follow you back to your tent."

I pointed at him. "That is your problem, Bruno. Not mine. You're the one who has an issue with my bloodline."

"No, I have an issue with you."

I crossed my arms. "Because you think I'm a liar."

"Mischief is a coyote's middle name."

"You're half-coyote, too."

His disgust about his were-father's bloodline showed on his face. "Not by choice."

God, he was such a jackass. I planted my hands on my hips. "What do you want from me? I swear I didn't kill Clint."

"Why did you leave?"

"Leave where?"

"My tent. You left in the middle of the night. When I went looking for you the next morning, you were gone."

I walked over and straightened my tarot cards. "I didn't want to see you leave." That was the honest truth.

"Why not?"

Because I didn't trust myself not to tell him the truth about my past crimes, my true identity, or my feelings for him. If I leaked any of those spicy bits it would only muck up the mess I'd already made of my life. Bruno didn't need to be dragged into my grand catastro-fuck. This was my penance to pay, not his.

"You might've gotten the wrong idea about us," I said.

His laugh sounded bitter. "What *us*? We had sex, most of which I can't even remember because I was falling-down drunk. There is no *us*."

I winced, even though his words were exactly what I'd been aiming to achieve with my buffering and continued withdrawal.

"Are you really here to find out who killed Clint?"

He nodded.

"Am I your only suspect?"

"Maybe." He pointed at the lock box where I'd put Ol' Blue. "I need your help."

I guffawed. "First you accuse me of killing my good friend and then you want my help?"

"I didn't accuse you of killing Clint, just questioned your whereabouts."

"Same difference."

"I've been ordered to seek your help."

"Ordered? By whom?"

"The owner. It appears your reputation for predicting the future has not escaped AC's attention."

"So, let me get this straight. You want me to help you figure out who killed Clint by using my abilities, while at the same time you suspect I could be the one behind his death?"

"Irony is a bitch, isn't it?"

Giving him the directions to Hell was on the tip of my tongue, but then I thought about Clint. If I could help bring his killer to justice, then I needed to put my emotions for Bruno aside and do whatever I could. Whoever murdered my friend needed to be drawn and quartered … or at least thrown in jail.

"Fine, I'll help you, but only because I loved Clint. He was a true friend and a wonderful person."

Bruno snorted. "I wouldn't go that far."

"What do you mean?"

"After digging into Clint's background, we found out some surprising news. It seems our clown friend had been placed in the circus to hide his true identity."

My pulse started to gallop. "Hide his identity?" That sounded a smidgeon familiar.

"Have you ever heard of the Gone Were program?"

I turned away so he couldn't see my cheeks turning red. "Gone Were?" I repeated, pretending to look for something in my trunk. I knew plenty about the organization that helped "Were-folks" disappear.

Bruno continued, "It's a witness protection program into which shapeshifters are placed when they've broken the law and turned state's witness against their criminal counterparts. Turns out Clint was part of that program."

I schooled my features, facing him. "You think that has something to do with Clint's murder?"

He nodded slowly, his dark eyes searching. "I don't think, I know."

"How can you be so sure?"

"Have you heard how Clint was killed?"

"Only that there was a knife involved."

His gaze hardened. "He was cut into pieces. Forty-eight pieces, to be exact."

Chapter Two

Later that evening, after the crowds had dispersed, I sat on the floor in my tent meditating. It was part of my nightly routine of cleansing my aura, removing any lingering attachments from the customers who'd paid me a visit. This was a ritual my grandmother had taught me as a young child under the wide western, star-dazzled sky.

How I missed those moments with her from so long ago when I'd lose myself in the sound of her chants. The breeze would rattle the mesquite trees next to her small abode, channeling through the canyon below in a long, sad howl that she claimed was an echo of our ancestors.

Thinking of the howling wind reminded me of the cries of sorrow during Clint's memorial. I sighed, my heart growing heavy with grief again.

I couldn't believe he'd been in the Gone Were program, just like me. What were the chances?

When I'd agreed to testify against my cousin and the crime boss he worked for, the attorney had sworn to me that I'd be tucked far away from those who might want to see me hanged from a tree. Gone Were had a good reputation for making witnesses of crimes disappear from the public eye, moving them safely out of harm's way. I'd signed on, knowing it was the only way to put my cousin away for good while saving my parents' welfare from being jeopardized along with mine.

Yet here I was with a dead friend who'd been part of the

same protection program. Was it a coincidence?

I stood up and stretched, my attention drifting from Clint to Bruno. Thoughts of the stubborn shifter had haunted me all evening. Those dark, dark eyes ever present during my visions, piercing the swirls of light and fog each time I sought Ol' Blue's advice.

How would I be able to work with Bruno day after day without giving in to my need for him? One time—one stupid time—I'd let my guard down and enjoyed the pleasure of his skin. I groaned at my foolishness. I should have never given in to the craving to touch. After months of resisting, I'd known a single taste would never satisfy, but he was supposed to leave the circus and my life for good, dammit.

I tugged out the pins that had secured my hair under the turban and veil I wore for my show and shook out my auburn curls. I pulled off my beaded satin tunic, checking for tears or loose threads before hanging it from a tent pole for tomorrow's show.

Bruno's brooding presence replayed in my head as I stepped out of my long, layered velvet skirt and shook the dust from it. One drunken mating and now the brute was mad at me for leaving him in the night. Of course he'd attributed it to his bias about me being an uppity purebred. Had I just been another piece of ass, would my disappearance come morning have mattered? Probably not. I had little doubt Bruno had enjoyed plenty of females before I came along. His skills in bed even while inebriated had proved his expertise at pleasuring the female body.

Damn it. Of all the shapeshifters out there, why did Bruno have to be my fated mate? And why did he have to come back into my world? Why couldn't Runash figure out who murdered Clint on her own? According to Ming and her big nose, Runash's resume and references were quite impressive. Apparently, they weren't good enough for the owner to let her solve Clint's murder on her own.

I grabbed my thigh-length robe from my bedchamber, sliding it on over my camisole and underwear. I'd have to be careful not to be in close proximity to Bruno for too long. There was only so much I could shield from him when we were in close range.

"Knock, knock," said a high-pitched voice.

I stepped back into my fortune-telling parlor. "Lemon Drop?"

The curtains parted, ushering in one of the petite, silver-haired contortionist identical twins. "No, it's Lolli Pop. I need your help, Electra."

Dagnabbit, I couldn't keep those two straight. I pointed to the chair across my parlor table. "Have a seat. How did your show go tonight?"

"Not so good." She lowered onto the chair, crossing her legs and arms, looking very pretzel-ish. "Lemon got stuck halfway through a tennis racket and I had to pull on her arm a little to get her loose. She says I tugged too hard and popped her shoulder out of joint, but I reminded her that in order to fit through the racket she has to pop her shoulder out of joint, so I just put it back into position."

I blinked, my tired brain trying to process that after a houseful of patrons needing to know everything from if any dead relatives would be crashing their All Hallow's Eve bash to the chances of finding their fated mates anytime this century.

"Was she able to shift and finish your act?"

Lolli's head bobble-nodded, her silvery blue eyes wide for such a late hour. "But she had trouble landing on her front paws in that last box. It's such a tight fit, you know."

I did know. I'd watched their act several times.

A mix of Siamese and Persian, Lemon Drop and Lolli Pop were left as tiny kittens in an orphanage in San Francisco's Chinatown. Since they came as a two-for-one deal and weren't purebred Persian or Siamese, parents were hard to come by. They ran away from the orphanage at the tender age of twelve and joined the circus, where the monkey brothers soon adopted them, sharing custody of the sweet girls. Now, ten years later, the two still lived with their adopted parents and traveled with us, contorting each night in their human form to fit through impossible obstacles. After they shifted into kitty cats, they performed an acrobatic ritual involving boxes that started out piled together like Russian stacking dolls. Their show was a big hit with the kids, especially with them in their adorable shapeshifter forms.

"What can I do for you tonight?" I asked.

Lolli stared down at her fingernails, frowning. "I think Lemon is sleeping with my boyfriend."

I resisted the urge to roll my eyes. "Not again." There seemed to be no limit to what the two girls shared.

"She's acting strange lately, and you know how Tom is."

Yeah, I did. Tom was a two-timing alley cat. Unfortunately, he was also an amazing trainer of the well-loved waltzing wildebeests and no other shifter could hitch a ride on their dancing backs around the big top ring without getting bucked off.

"Will you look at the tarot cards for me?" Lolli asked.

"Tonight?"

"I don't think I'll be able to sleep without knowing for sure."

"I already put my tarot cards away. How about I just use a deck of cards?"

"You can do that?"

"Sure. The different suits and cards each have meaning." I mixed up the deck of cards and spread them out before her. "Choose four." After she selected them, I flipped over the first. "Jack of hearts. That means you are continually in someone's thoughts."

Lolli giggled. "That must be Tom."

Or Lemon's since she was probably screwing around with her sister's boyfriend.

I turned over the second. "Ace of spades. That stands for the death of a friend."

"Do you think that means poor Clint?" she asked, her voice solemn.

"Probably." I flipped the third card. It was the ace of diamonds. "That means there is an important letter you need to read."

"What letter? A love letter? Tom always likes to slip me little love notes before my show."

The question was, what was Tom slipping her sister when Lolli wasn't looking?

I turned over the final card: Five of clubs. "You'll have a meeting soon with someone who will be interested in you."

"Oh, that's exciting. Who do you think it will be?"

Before I could answer, a gravelly voice answered from behind her. "Probably Ming," Bruno said, stepping into my parlor.

How had I not heard him coming? He must have snuck in using the age-old stealth ability most of us coyote shapeshifters possessed. He might despise his heritage, but I'd witnessed it serving him well in his career several times.

"She was looking for you earlier," he told Lolli. "She said she had a bonus check for some marketing work you've been doing for her."

Lolli leapt out of her chair with a squeal of pleasure and threw herself at him. "Bruno!" She hugged him, planting a kiss on his cheek. "Are you back for good?"

Bruno's dark gaze met mine. "Probably not."

"That's a bummer. You always make me feel safe when you're around."

Bruno made me feel safe, too, when I wasn't lusting after him like a fifteen-year-old groupie.

"Thanks for helping me tonight, Electra," Lolli said, blowing me a kiss good-bye. She squeezed Bruno's arm and then left us alone.

I collected my cards, stacking the deck on the table in front of me. "It's late, Bruno," I said without looking up.

He took Lolli's seat. Apparently, he was going to make

himself comfortable. "How do you remember all of the tricks?"

"What tricks?"

"The card stuff, for starters. There are fifty-two different answers you could've given her."

"You were eavesdropping." Crap, I needed to be more careful about picking up the sounds and smells of others with a possible murderer out there. Damn Bruno for clouding my senses.

"I was waiting my turn. It's not my fault I was born with excellent hearing."

I walked over to my narrow chest of drawers, packing away the cards, putting several feet of space between us. "I learned the different meanings long ago from my grandmother. She would test me often." Most of our time together was spent talking about the old ways, even older tricks of the trade, or methods to guide others in times of need.

"So you didn't just pull those out of your ass?"

"Contrary to what you believe, Bruno, I'm the real deal, with years of training under my belt."

His eyes narrowed in response, and then he glanced toward Ol' Blue's box. "If that's true, how about you get that tell-all ball of yours out and tell me what happened the night Clint died?"

"It doesn't work like that," I told him, staying put.

"How does it work then?"

"We make a connection first, usually a handshake will do, and then I look into it while you ask questions."

He held out his hand toward me.

"The questions have to be about you, not Clint." That wasn't the whole truth, but Bruno didn't need to know the secrets of my trade.

"Fine, I'll ask a few questions of my own then." He kept his hand out, waiting for me to take it.

The way he was staring at the belt of my silk robe made my mouth dry. Shit, after a long night of sifting through clients' thoughts and worries, my ability to shield my scent must be wavering.

I took a step backward, bumping into the tent wall behind me. "Not tonight, Bruno."

His mouth set into a thin line. He lowered his hand. "You're hiding something from me, Electra."

I was hiding a lot of things from him, including my real name. "Madam Electra" was the moniker Gone Were had given me when they'd dropped me off at the circus with my chest of clothes and Ol' Blue. I'd said good-bye to a quivering, skittish Nora Mai that day and sank into my Madam Electra role with nothing left to lose.

"Bruno, I'm too tired to fight with you. It's after midnight and we have an early start tomorrow afternoon. Come back in the morning to harass me."

He stood, closing the distance between us. I held still while his finger trailed down my cheek. "I remember bits and pieces of that night, Electra," he whispered. "Your beautiful eyes, honeyed lips, and soft skin haunt me."

I gulped, holding completely still. The urge to press against him filled me from head to toe.

"And when I dream," he said, leaning closer, sniffing my neck, "you're there with me, so wet and willing, crying out my name as I sink into you." He leaned back, his focus returning to my eyes. "But as soon as I wake up," he finished, snapping his fingers, "you disappear again."

I licked my dry lips. "We had a good time," I said huskily, breaking eye contact.

"Going out to the movies is a good time, Electra. We had sex, and if it was anything like my dreams, it was hot as hell. I passed out from the pleasure alone."

Goosebumps trailed down my arms at the memory of sensations during that intimate moment of flesh-on-flesh with him. He had passed out, but I hadn't been sure if it had been from sex or too much alcohol. "You were wasted, remember? You passed out from too much of the monkey brothers' hard cider."

"Bullshit. I've been drunk before. What you did to me was different. The sex was different."

"The sex was nice." I tried to sound apathetic about it. "But I'm not really your type, Bruno."

I could feel his gaze burning into me, but refused to meet his dark eyes. "You're right." He stepped back, giving me some much needed breathing room. "You're not my type, Electra. I don't like lying purebreds."

That stung, even though I deserved the slight right then. "We're back to name calling, are we?"

"For tonight we are." He walked toward the curtains, pausing to frown back at me. "Tomorrow, we'll start working together. Don't think you can run off and hide from me again, because I'm not leaving the circus until I figure out what you're hiding, and if it has anything to do with Clint's death."

Without another word, he left.

Trembling, I waited, my breath held in hopes that he'd return to bust down my barriers and make me his again. But he didn't. I heard his footsteps moving farther away.

Blowing out a breath of relief mixed with pent-up need, I pulled out Ol' Blue from the lock box. Somehow, I needed to find out who killed Clint pronto. If Bruno stood that close to me again tomorrow, I didn't know if I'd be able to keep my hands to myself.

The orb came to life as soon as I cleared my thoughts and touched my fingertips to it.

"Who killed the clown?" I whispered, peering down into the ball as the blue light and smoke swirled. After several seconds, through a thick haze, I saw myself laying out the cards for Lolli again.

Why was Ol' Blue showing me that?

I opened my mouth to ask the same question again, but then heard a scuffling sound in my waiting room. "Who's there?" I asked, stuffing Ol' Blue back in its box.

The curtains parted. "Hi, Electra."

Lolli was back. Was that what Ol' Blue had been trying to tell me? "I need to talk to you."

"What now, Lolli?"

"I'm not Lolli. I'm Lemon."

"Of course. Sorry about that. I'm so tired tonight I can't tell you two apart." Not that I ever could, even in broad daylight with a cup of coffee in me. "What can I do for you?"

"I think my sister is sleeping with my boyfriend," she started.

I groaned and pulled out my deck of cards again. If I had my way, the next time Tom shifted into an alley cat, I was going to drug him, take him to a local vet, and have him neutered, damn it.

Chapter Three

In the light of day, my predicament with Bruno didn't seem so dire.

Earlier, I'd climbed out of bed long enough to face the rising sun and chant the greeting my grandmother had taught me, then I'd fallen back onto my soft bed and slept another hour until I'd woken to the scent of coffee in the air.

Being a shapeshifter with a keen sense of smell had its advantages and drawbacks. A sniff of my armpits made me grimace, emphasizing a drawback of having a good nose.

A quick trip to the shared females' shower tent washed away the rank of yesterday's plights and last night's worries. I'd stopped at the monkey brothers' food stand on the way back to my tent, ordering a large cup of coffee to lubricate the grinding gears in my head. The morning air had warmed about fifteen degrees since I'd greeted the sun, requiring only my thigh-length robe and slippers to keep warm.

When I returned to my tent, I found I had a visitor waiting for me. Actually, he was more like a snooper.

"You could have waited outside," I told Bruno, glaring at him. He'd breached my fortune-teller parlor and was checking out the array of knickknacks on my chest of drawers, trinkets I'd acquired here and there during my months with the circus.

How long had he been in here? The whole time I was showering? How much had he poked around? Had he found my secret stash?

When he looked my way, his eyes got stuck on my bare legs. I set my coffee down on the parlor table next to Ol' Blue's stand.

"What are you wearing under that robe?" he asked.

"Why? Are we going to start this morning with a patdown? I can assure you I have no weapons hidden anywhere."

"I disagree. I've seen your breasts." He cocked his head. "At least I think I have." He shrugged. "Even if it's just a fantasy, I have an idea what you have under there and it's definitely a weapon."

"Why, Bruno Maska, I think that's the nicest thing you've ever said to me."

"I'm sure I said plenty of nice things during sex."

I turned away. The memories he was inspiring warmed me like the morning sun. "There was a lot of grunting," I said, trying to erect a roadblock on the direction this conversation was heading.

"I don't grunt during sex."

My smirk ran into his hard squint. "You do when you're drunk."

"I don't believe you."

Frowning, he picked up a picture of me kissing the cheek of a Bigfoot statue. Clint had taken that photo when we were doing a series of shows in Northern California. The laughs we'd shared still echoed in my head.

"Believe what you want," I said flippantly. "I was the more sober of the two of us."

He put the picture back and nailed me with a heated stare. "Why did you come back to my tent with me that night?" He rammed right through my roadblock attempt.

Damn it, why couldn't I have walked away that night and left things as they were—him hating my guts in plain sight and me lusting for him from the shadows?

I shrugged, pretending sex with him was no big deal. "We weren't fighting for once. Why not finish the night with some fun, right?"

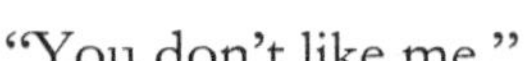

"You don't like me."

Wrong. "That's not entirely true."

"You've called me a lot of names over the last several months, most of them not very nice."

"That's because you make me mad with your purebred bias." Not to mention his doubt about my abilities as a psychic, but one issue at a time here. "Besides, you've called me a lot of names, too."

He came around the table, his eyes on my mouth. "Yeah, but I didn't mean them."

"Now who's the liar?" I held my ground as he closed the distance.

"Okay, maybe I meant one or two of them." He took me by the shoulders and pushed me back a couple of steps until my legs bumped against the edge of my chair. "But only when you were looking down your nose at me."

"I have never looked down my nose at you." I dropped onto the padded chair, glaring up at him.

His hands gripped the chair arms, imprisoning me. "The first time we met, you did."

I knew exactly where this was going. We'd rehashed it several times in our short but turbulent past. "No. You baited me with your damned questions as soon as you found out what I was and then purposely misinterpreted my responses."

"I distinctly remember the words that came out of your lips." His gaze iced over. "You said that mixed breeds are a testament to nature. That they defy description."

I huffed in his face. "That was meant as a good thing."

"Good? How?"

"You excel where I'm deficient due to my genetic lack of diversity."

His eyes drifted down over my robe. "You're not lacking in anything, Electra. Trust me."

"That's not the song you were singing the time you called me a liar and a fake in front of Clint and Eugene."

He stepped back, giving me breathing room. "I was referring to something else and you know it."

"Referring to what?"

"Us. This thing we have going on between us."

"We don't have anything," I lied.

"See, there you go again." He clenched his fists. "I'll give you this, though, I was wrong about the fake part. I may not remember much about the night we had sex, but I know there was no faking on your part. I can still feel your body clenching around me."

I stood and smoothed my robe over my thighs, remembering that moment with a flurry of stomach flutters. "Now you're just being crass." I tried to sound dismissive.

He rushed me, grasping my lapels, and hauled me against him. "I'm being honest." His lips came down on mine, taking out his anger on my mouth. I closed my eyes and waited out his frustration, holding myself wooden in spite of the urge to bury my fingers in his hair and give him a taste of what I needed from him.

"Kiss me," he ordered against my lips.

"Why?"

His lips left mine, trailing down my neck. "Because I missed you," he whispered when he reached my collarbone.

The pain and hunger in his response burned deep, searing my core. "Bruno," I said, gripping his shoulders as he pressed against me, making my head spin. "We can't do this again."

"Why not?" His mouth had reached my cleavage, his hands skimming up the back of my thighs.

"Because we have a murder to solve."

"This will only take a few minutes." His hand slipped under my robe, cupping my hip. "Jesus, you smell sweet and spicy, like molasses cookies." His mouth slid along the upper curve of my breast. "I want to bite your inner thigh."

God, no! If he bit me, I was toast. There was no way I could shield him even a little if he sank his teeth into me. A love nip

from a fated mate sealed the deal for life. I needed to put a stop to this, but …

"Electra!" a voice I'd grown to loathe called from the other side of the curtain.

"Fuck," I heard Bruno grumble, and then I was free.

I tugged my robe together, making myself decent again, and then pointed at the curtain that divided my parlor room from my bedchamber.

Bruno nodded and disappeared through the curtain.

"Come on through," I called, wishing I had taken the time to dress after my morning shower.

Ming angled through the curtain, carrying a big box. She nudged Ol' Blue's stand aside with the box and then set it down on my table.

"I'm supposed to leave this here."

"Says who?" I asked.

"Runash said Bruno requested I bring it to your tent."

"My tent?" Why *my* tent? Was he planning on staying here with me? Is that what this morning's attempt to sex me up was all about? If so, that was going to be a problem—a big, throbbing uncomfortable problem for both of us, but mainly me.

She sniffed the air. "I smell Bruno. Where is he?"

Dang her nose!

When Ming shifted, she was part Chinese Crested Dog and part Chihuahua, which made her loyal, tiny, and vicious. Since her loyalty was tied to her blog, which she used to promote AC's various branches of the circus, her viciousness came through on the page.

Rumor was that Ming had been sent to our freakshow division once AC saw her shift. The petite blond Barbie doll— minus the big boobs—morphed into a nearly hairless, tiny crossbreed with a few scraggly white-blond locks around her ears and needle-like sharp teeth. Kenneth, the master of ceremonies and Ming's lover, had recently let it slip that she was saving up for yet another round of plastic surgery after her last go with some magical hair tonic that had left her with hairy moles on her skin when she shifted.

I would have felt sorry for Ming if she wasn't such a little bitch. It seemed she had no morals when it came to writing, and her initial coverage on Clint's death was taken off the circus's website only after enough of us signed a petition to have it removed. Her second article almost caused several of us to walk away from the show, but Kenneth had come to his senses and forced her to take that one down as well. Now she was back for a third try, claiming this would be an uplifting epitaph, but my gut didn't trust her one bit.

"Bruno was here earlier," I explained. "He stepped out to grab something to eat." I opened the box lid. "What is this stuff?"

"It's Clint's remains. Well, not his remains, but the things from his tent. After he died, we packed them up and set it all aside in case any relatives came looking for his belongings."

From the box, I pulled out an alarm clock with an ugly goat version of a chupacabra on it and felt a sob rise in my throat. I'd bought Clint the clock as a joke because he kept showing up late to our morning coffee date. Clint started my days with a smile, always turning up with his clown makeup in place, making funny faces while drinking across from me. How could someone have laid a hand on him, dammit? The world needed more happy clowns these days, not fewer.

The clock wasn't moving. The batteries must have died. I set it aside and rifled through the rest of the box's contents. His metal skates still had the clown shoes attached to them. Eugene should probably keep those along with the skate key. Under the shoes was a mix of everyday clothes, a couple of razors, his wallet, a tin cup from Mt. Rushmore, and a collection of what looked like flotsam and jetsam, washed in from the sea.

Suddenly aware of my audience, I closed the lid and hid my pain behind a tight smile. "I'll be sure to give this to Bruno."

"Is he back to stay?" she asked.

"I'm not sure, why?" Did she want to write about that in her fucking blog?

She shrugged. "He's nice to have around. Easy on the eyes, you know."

Yeah, I knew. It was my turn to shrug. "Sure, if you like his type."

"Oh, I do," she said, licking her lips.

As if I needed another reason not to like the little bitch. "You know about his condition, right?"

"What condition?"

I covered my mouth. "Oh, I wasn't supposed to tell anyone about that. Forget I mentioned it."

Her eyes sparkled with curiosity. "You can tell me. I won't write about it, I swear."

I opened my mouth like I was going to blab, but then pinched my lips together. "No, I promised I wouldn't tell a soul. He'd kill me if I told anyone." I walked over and held one of the curtains back. "Thanks for bringing this. If we find out anything about Clint's murder, Bruno will be sure to let you know."

Ming paused next to me on her way out. "You're helping him?"

I didn't think that was a secret, not if Bruno had told someone to have Clint's box brought to my tent. "Yes. AC ordered Bruno to deputize me on this case."

She made a funny face that sort of resembled a frown, but thanks to her last Botox injection, it looked more like the circus's vet had shoved a thermometer up her ass. "But Bruno thinks you're a fake."

A fire lit in my belly. Maybe I should tell Ming that Bruno, the big butthead, had the mange. Better yet, heartworms. I took a breath, reining in my temper. "AC believes in me, though, and you know what we say in the circus, what AC wants …"

"AC gets, no matter who she has to mow down in the process," Ming finished.

Well, something like that. "Exactly. Now, if you don't mind, I need to get dressed." I ushered her toward the waiting room.

Ming made it as far as the outer tent flap. "Oh, one more thing, Electra."

"What's that?"

"What do you know about the Gone Were program?"

I flinched, hiding my reaction with a fake sneeze. "Damned allergies," I said, dabbing under my nose. "Gone Were program? What's that?"

"It was a program Clint was part of, I hear. No biggie if you haven't." She smiled, but there was something ugly in her kohl-lined eyes. "Give Bruno a hug for me and tell him I've missed him around here this last month."

I glared poison darts after her as she walked away. When I turned back to my parlor room, Bruno stood behind my chair with his arms crossed.

"My condition?" A muscle ticked in his jaw.

I grinned sheepishly. "Sorry about that, but you don't need her hanging on you."

"Why not?"

"She's trouble."

"And you're not?"

I walked over and picked up the alarm clock, flipping it over. "I'm a good girl."

He moved to the table next to me, opening the box of Clint's belongings. "You're part right on that one."

While Bruno fished through the box, I used my thumbnail to unscrew the back cover of the clock. I had batteries around here somewhere.

"What are you doing with that?" he asked.

"Making it work again."

"Why?" He set the roller skates on the floor.

"Because I want to keep it."

"Why?" he asked again.

I shot him a frown. "Because it reminds me of Clint."

The back popped off and a piece of folded paper fell out onto the floor. I set the clock down and bent to pick it up, figuring it for the instructions. When I unfolded it, my whole body went rigid. A small squeak escaped my lips. A vision flashed before my eyes, violent and bloody, filled with screams of pain. Pieces of flesh were everywhere. Something was missing, though, something taken from the scene after Clint stopped moving. I could feel it.

"Do you think …" Bruno started to say and then stopped. His hand warmed my shoulder a second later. "Electra, what is it?"

When I didn't answer, he took the paper from my hand, reading it.

I stumbled over to my chair and fell into it, my legs trembling. Holy shit!

Stars swam around the edge of my vision. I lowered my head between my knees, taking several deep breaths.

"Electra," Bruno said, kneeling in front of me. "Talk to me."

"That's a contract."

"I know."

"On Clint's head."

"Yes."

I looked up at him. "How was Clint killed?"

He hesitated, searching my eyes. "I told you he was sliced to pieces."

"Yes, but you left something out, didn't you?"

He ran his fingers through his hair. "Listen, Electra."

"Just tell me, dammit!"

"I don't think—"

"Which piece of him was missing?"

Bruno reared, his mouth open. "How do you know about that?"

Because I knew all about bounty hunters and their fucked-up tricks. Before I'd been placed at the circus by the Gone Were program, they'd trained us on how to detect a bounty hunter kill from a regular murder. "Which piece?" I asked again.

"Clint's right index finger." Bruno watched me closely, trying to see through my poker face. "Runash thinks a stray dog or cat found it and ate it for dinner."

Runash might be the current head of security with all manner of impressive credentials, but Runash was wrong. Clint's index finger was the trophy needed to collect the bounty on his head.

If Clint's killer had been a bounty hunter, did that mean I was next on the hit list?

Chapter Four

We need to talk to Finn," I told Bruno. I left him standing in my fortune-teller parlor with a frown on his face, closing the curtains to my private quarters behind me.

I glanced around at the clothes strewn all over my bed, the makeup scattered on my travel case that I used as a nightstand, and the romance novel propped like a tent on my pillow. Eugene kept a library of his favorite love stories, and ever since Bruno had left I'd been easing my pining for him with steamy romances.

What had Bruno thought as he stood in here while I was shooing off Ming? Had he gone through my stuff, searching for more evidence that tied me to Clint? Had he scanned through the sex scene I'd bookmarked in the novel?

"Why Finn?" he asked through the closed curtain, making me jump into action.

"Because he was Clint's best friend." Pushing aside my angst about Bruno standing in my lair, I changed into a long red skirt and a white peasant blouse. "He might have a few answers."

Slipping into a pair of strappy sandals, I fluffed my damp curls in the mirror. I paused long enough to pinch some color into my pale cheeks and apply a layer of prickly-pear fruit lip balm, thinking of one of my grandmother's favorite sayings: *You can take the coyote out of the desert, but you can't take the desert out of the coyote.*

Bruno was still going through the contents of Clint's box

when I stepped out from my bedchamber. He looked my way and did a double take, his eyes darkening.

"Let's go." I grabbed my bag of rune stones from my chest of drawers. "It's still early, but Finn should be awake by now."

Bruno reached for me as I passed by him, but I dodged his hand. "Come back here, woman." He chased me out into the sunlight.

I knocked his hand away when he tried to snag me again. "Bruno, focus."

He scrubbed his hands over his face and then shook his head. "Damn it, what is wrong with me?"

Some called it "love-lust" and others called it "the shine." It was a condition that was known to take over a shapeshifter when their fated mate was near but out of reach.

I needed an hour alone to regroup and focus my energy into strengthening the buffer between us, but with Bruno next to me every minute, I could barely keep my own emotions under control.

He scowled down at me as we passed the big top tent on our way to Finn's place over near Clown Alley. "Did you put some kind of spell on me?"

"I'm not a witch and you know it."

"It would be so much easier if I could go back to being pissed at you 24/7."

"Have you ever analyzed why that is?"

I caught sight of Eugene between two of the tents. He was in his bear form trying to flick a lighter with his huge bear paw. When his snout lifted, sniffing in our direction, I waved at him. "Everything looks good for this afternoon's show," I called, giving him a thumbs-up.

He watched me with round, worried bear eyes until we were out of sight.

"Analyzed what?" Bruno asked. "Why you made me want to snarl and growl whenever you came near?"

"Yes." We rounded a green and yellow striped tent and found

the man of the hour … make that the jackrabbit. "Good morning, Finn," I said, smiling down at the large *Leporid*.

Finn preferred to stay in his jackrabbit form most of the time, even off stage. He changed into a human only when decorum required it. He could speak clearly no matter his form, something many shifters weren't able to do.

The jackrabbit lowered his tanning mirror. Raising his sunglasses, he squinted up at me from his lawn chair. "Electra, you're looking quite brilliant," he said in his fake British accent. His long ears flicked away a fly, his amber gaze moved to the man next to me. "Good day, mate," he said to Bruno, changing to an Australian accent. "I heard you'd returned to our ranks."

"Only temporarily," Bruno told him, reaching out to bump fists with Finn's rabbit paw. "You're practicing for tonight's show, I see."

"Aye, laddie," he said with a Scottish turn.

Finn the Jackrabbit sold out every single night with both the old and young. His act was quite simple and yet amazing. He would sit on stage in a high-backed, green leather reading chair. Next to him on a nightstand was a single glass of water. In his hand was a thick book of quotes he'd compiled himself from his idol—Bugs Bunny. In various accents from around the world, he would read the quotes, sometimes standing to act out a line or two of his monologue.

His ability to spellbind a crowd was known throughout many circuses. With words alone, he could bring tears of laughter or heart-wrenching sadness. I'd sat in on his show a couple of times recently to keep my mind off the loss of Clint. I glanced at the man standing beside me. Finn's show had also distracted me from longing for Bruno.

Finn leaned down and grabbed a hand-rolled cigarette from the ashtray at the foot of his lawn chair and lit up, puffing perfect smoke rings into the air. Correction, I thought, smelling the sweet odor of marijuana, make that a joint.

"You'd better be careful with that," Bruno said, pointing at the joint. "You know Kenneth is always worried about being raided for drugs by local law enforcement."

Finn waved him off. "This is Tinkerville, dude." He slipped into surfer mode, his dialect of choice. "It's a shifter's paradise. Weed is only non-copacetic in the human world."

"Bruno's been living in the human world too long," I told Finn, grinning. "He's forgotten how life at the circus is for us lowlifes."

"His loss, man." Finn offered me a toke, but I shook my head.

"I need a clear head for this afternoon's crowd." I glanced around to make sure we had no eavesdroppers. "We need to ask you a few questions."

"Did you bring the stones?"

I held up the bag.

Finn was a bit superstitious. He believed that if he had to answer more than three questions in a row, he'd lose his voice. I'd once joked about holding onto his "rabbit" foot when he answered and been ordered out of his tent for my lousy sense of humor.

Clint, being intuitive, had figured out a way to appease Finn on this subject. For every question asked of him, I had to read one of my rune stones. It made no sense to me per my teachings about the runes, since the stones are about searching for possible causes and effects and then finding possible outcomes for whoever casts the stones, but I'd gone along with it since it eased Finn's worries.

Thanks to the stones, Finn had been able to move past his superstition and interact more with others, making him a happy rabbit.

I closed my eyes, trying to find a neutral state, but with Bruno standing beside me, and a circus full of people milling nearby, I was lucky to find a somewhat calm location. I pulled three stones from the bag and set each stone down next to Finn's ashtray, lining them up.

"Okay." I turned to Bruno. "I need a question about the past."

"The night Clint was killed, did you see anyone around that you didn't recognize? Any strangers?"

I started with the rune at the far left that focused on past actions or situations, asking the question word for word.

"Necessity. Shadow," I read the stone, looking up at Finn. "Friction."

He nodded, accustomed to playing this game with me. He paused to take a hit off his joint before blowing out a lungful and speaking. "I was on my way back from the shower and saw someone in a hooded jacket sneaking around behind the big top tent."

That really didn't get us anywhere.

I looked at Bruno. "Ask a question about our present situation."

"Why can't I ask another about the shadow figure?"

"Because that's not how the stones and Finn work."

Bruno growled. "Fine. Let's see. Has anyone else come around asking about Clint's whereabouts or circumstances involving his death?"

"That's sort of two questions," I said.

"Just ask," he said, pointing at the stones.

I did and focused on the second stone. "Death. Dreaming. Magic."

Finn thumped his long hind paw on the ground a couple of times while taking another toke. "Ming has come by several times, digging for what I know about Clint's past."

Damn Ming and her freaking blog.

"Runash," he said, looking up at Bruno. "She was supposed to fill your shoes, right, dude?" At Bruno's nod, Finn continued, "She came by with all sorts of questions after they took Clint's body away."

If it was in pieces, I tried not to imagine how horrific that process must have been.

"That's all I can think of at the moment, besides the usual gossipy shit from everyone around, but that doesn't count."

I pointed at the stones. "The final question needs to be about a future situation."

"This is crazy," Bruno said.

"You wanted *my* help, remember?"

"No, I was ordered to ask for your help."

"Fine, I'll ask." I focused on calming my thoughts again, taking a step away from Bruno to help. "Will we find Clint's killer at the circus?"

I read the third stone. "Fertility. True Love. Harmony."

Bruno snorted in disgust. "Well, that's about as far from an answer to that as we can get."

Finn stared up at me, his long whiskers twitching. His gaze moved to Bruno, and then back. "There's your answer."

My heart quickened. How could Finn know that Bruno was my true love? I started to shake my head to deny it.

"Harmony, dudette." He pointed his joint at Bruno. "You two need to stop bickering and in the harmony you'll find the answers to Clint's murder."

"Finn!" Kenneth the ringmaster called from somewhere nearby.

"Shit!" Finn stubbed out his joint on the lawn chair and tucked it in his pocket. "I need to scram. Kenneth's on the warpath today, and I don't need him disrupting my karma flow, man."

Karma flow? I collected my rune stones.

He hopped away faster than I could run in my human form, zigzagging between tents. I turned to face Kenneth and his wrath, but Bruno tugged me into a nearby tent, putting his finger over my lips.

We waited as Kenneth stomped past, still hollering Finn's name. When he was safely past, I whispered, "Why are we hiding from Kenneth?"

"Because he's one of my suspects. I don't want him finding

out who I've talked to about Clint."

"Kenneth is a suspect?" I crossed my arms. The guy was a gentle soul most days, at least when he wasn't hunting down pot-smoking jackrabbits. "He's a werepug, for crissake." And quite an adorable wrinkly-faced guy when he shapeshifted with one hell of a vertical jump for his size, which he once told me was because his father was a Jack Russell terrier. "Everyone knows werepugs aren't killers. They might lick you to death, but unless Clint was having sex with Ming behind Kenneth's back, I can't see any reason he'd have for hurting the clown."

"Kenneth wasn't in his tent the night Clint died. He and Ming had a fight and he'd walked out."

"Maybe he went into town to drink away his frustrations. Hell, if I was sleeping with Ming, I'd drink every damned night."

"Kenneth's lack of alibi puts him on my list of suspects." Bruno's tone made it clear that was the end of that discussion.

"Who else is on your list beside Kenneth and me?"

His jaw tightened. "That's for me to know."

I poked him in the chest. "If we're going to work together, you need to start sharing information."

His eyes dipped to my mouth. "I'll tell you what. For every kiss you give me, I'll give you a name."

I rolled my eyes. "Are you for real?"

He shrugged. "It was worth a shot."

"Forget it." I walked out, heading toward my own tent.

Bruno caught up with me. "You're no fun."

"Ha! Since when have you ever been fun?"

"I've always been fun, ask around."

"No, you've always been bossy, brooding, and snappy."

"Only around you."

"Lucky me."

"I can't help it. You drive me nuts."

"Because I'm a purebred, I know," I finished for him. I slipped inside my tent, striding through the curtain into my parlor.

He followed. "No, because you're too good for me."

"Says who?"

"All of the other purebred dickheads."

I sighed. "You really need to get over this issue you have with breeding. I can't help who my parents are, just like you can't."

He paced in front of my parlor table a couple of times, and then turned. "What were your parents' names?"

"What? Why?" Where had that question come from?

His eyes searched my face. "Who's N.M.?"

"What?"

"N.M." He pointed toward my inner chamber. "It's on that little wooden heart on your nightstand."

I folded my arms. "You were snooping."

"You kept yapping with Ming. I got bored while I sat on your bed and waited."

There was no way I could answer him honestly. If I told him my real name, I wouldn't be able to shield myself emotionally or on paper. He could look me up and find out about my crime-laden past. Then he'd be doubly disgusted, both with my secret and with his attraction to a woman who'd once worked for one of the biggest crime bosses in the desert Southwest.

"It stands for New Mexico."

"You're lying."

"I'm not. Take a look at any dictionary and it will tell you that N.M. is the two-letter abbreviation for 'New Mexico.' "

His jaw tightened. "I know the fucking abbreviation for New Mexico, Electra." He closed the distance between us, tipping my chin up, forcing me to look him in the eyes. "What I really want to know is, who's Nora Mai?"

Shit! I gulped.

Where had he found my real name?

Chapter Five

I don't know who that is," I straight out lied. I had to, because telling him the truth would fuck up our lives both in and out of the bedroom.

Bruno wasn't buying my song and dance. I could see disbelief in his eyes. "You know how I can tell you're lying right now?"

I kept still, fighting to keep my face blank and breathing regular. Rather than answer, I raised one eyebrow.

"I can hear your heart racing," he answered.

"What can I say? You make me nervous, especially when we're alone."

He leaned closer, his cheek grazing mine as he inhaled next to my ear. "I can smell your fear."

"I'm afraid Clint's killer might return." That was the full-on truth.

His fingers trailed down my arms, locking onto my wrists. "I can feel you tremble."

I decided to sidetrack him. "Fine. You figured me out, Mr. Security Head Honcho. I am hiding something. I'm hiding that I want you again. Happy now?"

If I could just keep him from finding out my real identity a little longer, I could finish tonight's show, pack up, and leave when everyone was sleeping. I didn't want to say good-bye to my circus family, but this place was too dangerous now that I knew Clint had been in the Gone Were program and a bounty hunter most likely killed him.

Bruno growled and stepped back. "Don't play your wicked games with me, woman."

"I told you before, I'm not a damned witch. I don't play 'wicked' anything."

"Right. You're a cunning trickster who lies for a living."

He was goading me, I could tell, but I'd grown up being poked by bullies about coyote folklore. "None of that seemed to bother you the night you took me to your bed."

He sat on the edge of my parlor table, his arms crossed. "You probably drugged me."

His words made me want to whop him upside the head. "I did not drug you, you big bonehead." I pointed at the curtains. "Get out of my tent, Bruno, or I'm going to hit you with something."

"I'm not leaving until you tell me who Nora Mai is."

"Then it looks like you're going to become a permanent fixture in my tent." I smirked. "I hope you don't mind if I drape you in beads so you match the rest of the furniture."

"Let me help you with your memory," he said. "Nora Mai died a little over a year ago of exposure and dehydration while hiking in a remote canyon in southeastern Utah. Her body was found a month later by a group of photographers out on a day trip. Her remains were well-picked over by that time, with her dental records being the only way to positively identify her." He shook his head. "That southwestern sunshine, not to mention the vultures, does a real number on an exposed body."

I walked over to my chest of drawers, pulling out a few tricks of the trade for this afternoon's early opening. "Sounds like a tragic way to go out," I said when my back was to him. Not to mention lonely and sad.

I'd had such high hopes as a young girl, planning to use my grandmother's teachings to help lost and lonely souls. Instead, here I sat in my tent every night, spinning tales of happiness and mystery for one stranger after another, barely using the gifts with which I was born.

"According to one of the articles I read, Nora's parents were devastated at the news, their grief driving them to leave the country entirely to escape her memory."

My eyes pricked, tears threatening at the mention of my parents. The only way to keep them safe was to let them think I was dead. I wasn't allowed to learn where they'd gone after a fake counselor from Gone Were had urged them to relocate in order to better deal with the loss of their only child.

I'd made a wrong choice, and it had destroyed not just my own life, but my parents' too. The self-loathing I'd lived with for many, many moons resurfaced, making my chest ache again, the wound re-opened.

I cleared my throat. "I told you, I don't know who this Nora Mai woman is."

"Clint seemed to."

My breath caught. "He did?" I tried to keep the quivering I felt clear to my fingertips out of my voice.

"Her name was written on the back of a circus flier we found in his tent."

What flier? Why my name? Who had written it? Clint? Someone else? Someone who knew about the bounty on my head?

"That's intriguing," I said in a pseudo-bored tone.

"Very intriguing, especially considering that it was one of the fliers Ming had made up advertising your services."

Ahhh, so that was why Bruno was sniffing at my door, throwing my real name around, fishing for reactions.

I was more concerned about how Clint had come across my real name. Had he been looking into my past, or had someone else been asking him about it?

No matter the answer, I had to leave as soon as tonight's show was over. I'd take Ol' Blue and whatever else I could fit in one bag and catch the next bus out of town. Better yet, I'd hitch a ride on a freight train. That would leave even less of a trail.

"Electra," Bruno said, drawing my gaze. "Tell me."

I tried to smile. "There's nothing to tell."

He came closer. "Tell me," he said again.

"I don't know why Clint would have a flier of mine with that name. It must be a weird coincidence."

He took the deck of cards from my hand. "Tell me."

The temptation to lean into him and hide my face in his broad chest tugged on me.

My fated mate. I sighed, shaking my head. Why now? Why here? Why Bruno?

His hands framed my face, tipping it up to his. "Who is Nora Mai?"

If I told him and then disappeared with the wind …

"This Nora Mai's death might be somehow connected to Clint's killer," he said. "If you have any information on her, you need to help me for Clint's sake."

Had my trail led the killer to Clint? Was his death my fault? My heart ached for the poor clown. "Nora Mai's death has nothing to do with Clint's murder," I whispered.

His lids lowered into a squint. "How do you know?"

My guilt and fear won the game of tug-of-war in my head. I was in over my head. Before I ran off into the night, Bruno deserved to know the truth about how I might or might not fit into Clint's murder. "Because I'm Nora Mai."

His eyes widened, his hands falling away. "You are …" He took a step back, his face pale. "Why?"

That one word opened so many doors. I walked over to the curtain leading to the waiting room, peeking out to make sure we had no eavesdroppers. Then I returned and grabbed his arm, hauling him into my bedchamber.

"Years ago I got caught up in an ugly, sticky mess," I said in a hushed voice. "My cousin came to me needing me to look into Ol' Blue to help him find his girlfriend who he feared had been kidnapped. At least that was his sob story. He offered to pay me for my help. I was young, believed his angst was legit, and took his money. What I saw in my ball helped him find her.

"Only it turned out it wasn't his girlfriend, but rather a woman who had betrayed him. A couple of days later, she turned up dead in the desert because of my naiveté. I was unsure if I should go to the police, worried they might pin the crime on me somehow since I was related to him."

"Electra," he started, then corrected himself. "Nora, you were innocent."

I held up my hand to stop him. "There's more. My cousin returned a few days after that, this time looking for an old friend. I told him I wasn't going to help. He informed me then that he was a hit man for one of the local crime ringleaders. Then he held up a picture of my parents and told me that if I didn't help him find this guy, he would shoot both of my parents in the head."

Bruno sucked air between his teeth. "Fuck."

"Exactly." I grimaced. "My cousin promised this was the last time he'd ask for my help and offered me a big sum of money. I figured I could use the money to get away from him, but when I approached my parents about leaving the country with me, they didn't want to go. They'd grown up in the Southwest and couldn't imagine living anywhere else. I thought about telling them the truth about my cousin, but I decided their ignorance might be for the best in this case."

I wrung my sweaty hands, remembering the fear and worry that I'd lived with during those dark days. "As you can imagine, it went downhill from there. My cousin kept coming back each month with a new missing person he needed me to find, promising it was the last time, paying me well each time. I told myself the people I found were criminals and probably had earned their fate, but deep down I knew better. My gift was supposed to be used to help, not kill. After a year of being manipulated and threatened at every turn, I knew I had to do something to stop him or I'd never be free."

"So you turned him into the police and faked your death?"

"Basically. My death was one of the requirements for me to

enter the Gone Were program. In order to become Madam Electra, Nora Mai had to die a public death."

"Your parents weren't in on it?"

I shook my head. "They think I'm dead."

He frowned. "So, that's your tie to Clint."

I nodded even though it wasn't a question. "But I didn't realize Clint was part of the program until you told me." I chewed on my lower lip. "Apparently, he knew about me, though." I wondered if that was why he had been so kind to me from the start. Had Gone Were leaked my true identity to him? Was I put here under his watchful eye? He certainly made a point of keeping track of me each day, something I'd assumed was just friendly in nature. After all, Clint had kept tabs on everyone.

Bruno rubbed his jaw. "Was Clint's death tied to you somehow? Or was it just happenstance that a bounty hunter came for him without realizing you were here, too?"

"I've been asking myself that since you told me about Clint being in the program."

"No wonder you've been so skittish."

"Wouldn't you be if you were in my shoes? I was supposed to be safe here. Gone Were promised that if I did my part and put that bastard behind bars, they'd keep me alive."

"Shit," he said, looking around my tent. "We need to put you somewhere safer than this place. Someone could sneak in here and kill you as easily as they did Clint."

"It doesn't matter." I decided to be open about my plans. "I'm leaving after tonight's show."

His mouth tightened. "You're going to run away? How coyote of you."

"Screw you, Bruno. I have to go. If I stay here and the bounty hunter finds me, I'm putting everyone around me at risk." Especially Bruno.

"I won't let you leave."

"It's not your choice."

"I can protect you."

"Like you protected Clint?"

He winced. "That's not fair. I wasn't here."

"You can't be everywhere at once, Bruno. If I leave, you can see if anyone else disappears to follow my trail. If they do, you'll know who killed Clint."

"Bad idea. If the killer follows, you are even more at risk and the criminal escapes our grasp."

Those were two good points, damn it. "What, then? You want me to stay and be your bait?"

"I can keep you safe, Elect ..." he stopped, correcting himself again. "Nora."

"It's not going to work."

"You underestimate me. I may not be a purebred like you, but I can still protect you."

I hated the frustration and hurt I heard in his tone. He didn't understand that my reasoning had nothing to do with who his parents were. It went deeper than that.

"Bruno, you being a mixed breed has nothing to do with it." My heart thumped so loudly in my chest he had to be able to hear it. "There is something else I've been keeping from you."

His eyes searched mine. "You're not really a purebred?"

"No, that's true. I'm a full werecoyote." I cringed in anticipation of my next blow. "I'm also your fated mate."

He blinked, his head cocking to the side. "That's not possible."

"Why not?"

"Fated mates aren't real. They're fiction. Something they write about in those romance books Eugene and you read."

"Fated mates are real, Bruno. They just aren't always easy to find. Unfortunately for you, yours has a history of lying to save her fur." I gave him a crooked smile. "And she's a purebred with psychic abilities."

He shook his head. "I don't believe it."

"Have you not been fixated with me since that first day we met?"

"Yeah, but that was because you were stealing from the monkey brothers' food stand."

"Oh, come on. How many times do I have to tell you that I wasn't stealing? They told me I could have two frozen chocolate bananas because I was new."

"The monkey brothers are never that generous."

I threw my hands up. "You're impossible."

"And you've done nothing but lie to me from the start."

"To protect you."

He continued shaking his head. "I'll admit I've been interested in you since that first time I found you stealing, but this thing between us is merely sexual attraction."

"It's more than sexual attraction, trust me."

His gaze hardened. "What's your game here? Are you playing up this fated mate thing in order to throw me off track somehow?"

"Damn it, Bruno. After months of shielding my scent from you, I finally come clean and you think I'm playing some fucking trick." I bared my teeth at him, imagining giving the hard-headed shifter a love nip right on the ass. That would teach him a thing or two about fated mates and pissing me off. "Do you think I want to have the one individual in this world I'm destined to love be *you*? I thought St. Bernard shifters were supposed to be loyal and loving." I played on his loyalty to his mother's were-breed to give him some of his own medicine. "All I've gotten from you since day one was distrust and snarls."

"I'm sorry I'm not more purebred for you, princess," he snapped back.

That was it. I'd had enough of this shit. "Get the hell out of my tent."

He didn't budge. "Prove it."

"Prove what?"

"You say you've been hiding your scent so I wouldn't know you're my fated mate. Prove it. Make me believe fated mates exist."

"If this is some stupid trick to get me to have sex with you again ..."

"I'm not looking for sex here, woman. I want the truth. I'm tired of being tricked and played by you. Show me something real."

"Fine. Give me a second." I turned my back to him, closing my eyes, focusing inward. One by one, I lowered what was left of the buffers I'd fixed between us, allowing my energy to flow freely, pure and straightforward.

I turned back to him. He stood where I'd left him.

I didn't say a word. Instead, I focused on him, his strength, his loyalty, his big heart that kept him tangled up in everyone's business. In return, I let him see the real me, lonely, sad, hungry for his love.

Holding out my hand, I said in a husky voice, "It's nice to meet you, Bruno Maska. I'm Nora Mai."

He dragged his gaze from my face, frowning down at my hand. Slowly, carefully, he reached out and took it. Energy sparked when our skin touched, heat flaring up my arm. Lust ran rampant through me, busting down any last remaining barriers between us. My love for him flooded my core, sending me hurtling toward a meltdown.

When his attention returned to my face, his cheeks were flushed, his eyes black with need. His breath picked up speed, his grip on my hand tightening.

"Do you feel it now?" I asked.

"You've been blocking *this* all along?" At my nod, he asked, "How?"

"It's a trick my grandmother taught me long ago. The original purpose was to shield me from danger, but when it came to you, it was the only thing I could find that seemed to work."

He pulled me toward him, his intent clear on his taut face. "I want to taste you."

"Bruno, stop."

"You don't understand. I have to. Now."

"I *do* understand. I've been living with this for months, remember? Why do you think I've been reading Eugene's books?"

"How many?" He slid one hand around to my lower back, pressing me against him.

Oh, hell. I could feel his need, smell his desire, hear the lust in his voice. "How many what?"

"How many books?" His mouth lowered to mine.

"A lot," I whispered, lost in his eyes.

"You should have shown me before now. I could have been taking care of you all along, both in and out of bed."

"I'm a wanted woman," I said, trying one last time to stop him.

"I know. I've wanted you since the first time I saw you."

"Bruno, you can't protect me. I have to leave."

"Not without me." His mouth came down on mine, his hands spanning my hips.

I wrapped my arms around his neck, plastering myself against him, like I had that night a month ago when I'd given into the love-lust. I sucked his tongue into my mouth, tasting him, teasing him, while my hips moved against his.

"I knew it," he said in between kisses that were growing more frenzied by the second.

"Knew what?"

"I kept dreaming about you." He kissed along my jaw. "About that night." His teeth grazed my earlobe. "I couldn't get you out of my head. I knew it was more than just great sex." His hands slid up under my blouse, his fingers climbing my ribs. "But it was all so muddled in my head come daylight. I was going nuts, wanting you like crazy and not understanding why."

I unfastened his jeans, even though we needed to stop. It was broad daylight and the circus gates would open any minute. "Say my name," I ordered, sliding my hand inside his open zipper.

He kissed along my collarbone, his thumbs exploring my curves through my camisole. "Nora," he said, his voice ragged with lust as I touched him.

I moaned in pleasure at the sound of it on his lips alone. There'd be no walking away from this now. Not without a shattered heart and way too many tears.

He lifted my shirt and bent down, taking me in his mouth through my satin camisole. "Bruno," I gasped, squeezing and rubbing him with the heel of my palm. "I want—"

"Hello?" a voice called from the other side of the curtain. "Madam Electra, are you in here?"

Bruno froze, his forehead wrinkling. *Runash*, he mouthed the name of the head of security.

Shit! There was no hiding from her in a tent. Besides, she'd be able to smell me. Runash was a cougar shapeshifter. She could smell a mouse eating cheese on the other side of the big top tent.

I stepped back from Bruno, adjusting my clothes. "I'll be right out," I hollered to Runash.

"I just need a few minutes of your time," she said.

I heard her sniffing and frowned at Bruno. His scent was hard to miss, and now it would be all over me.

"What's this about?" I called, grabbing a bottle of perfume and spritzing my neck, chest, and skirt. I sprayed in the air several times for good measure, making Bruno cringe and wave his hand in the air.

"Just a question or two," Runash said.

I stepped through the curtain, smiling at the newest security chief. She took her job seriously, keeping her hair short in a military-style cut and wearing the word SECURITY down her thigh, on her camp shirt, and across her hard-brimmed hat.

"What questions?" I asked, taking up my tarot cards to keep my hands busy.

She sniffed again, frowning toward the curtain I stepped through. "Your relationship with Clint the Clown."

Chapter Six

"Did I interrupt something?" Runash asked, nudging her chin toward the curtain leading to my private quarters.

"No. Bruno is looking through some of Clint's stuff from the box Kenneth sent over." I lied smoothly, because while she might have a better sense of smell, I was a professional trickster. "I moved him behind the curtain because we're opening early today, as you know."

She nodded, sitting down in the chair reserved for paying clients. "I'd prefer we have this meeting in private."

Bruno stepped out from my bedchamber, his face set. "Why would I need to leave, Runash?" he asked in lieu of a greeting. "You and I are both set on finding the same answer—who killed Clint."

"Yes, but judging from the scent in the air, Electra has swayed you into believing she is innocent."

My neck warmed at her hint at the smell of sex in the air. Rather than deny the truth, I owned up to it. "There wasn't any swaying necessary. Bruno and I have been lovers for a while now."

Her dark blond eyebrows climbed up her forehead. "You two have been keeping secrets," she accused.

"Our private life is nobody's business," Bruno said with a calm I didn't feel myself. "If you believe my relationship with Electra compromises my ability to find Clint's killer, you'll need to take that up with the owner. In the meantime, I'll remind you that not only did the owner advise me to seek Electra's counsel, but that I am lead on this murder case. Your role is only to assist me, as needed."

Runash's lids lowered into a menacing glare for a moment, then she blinked it away and gave him a brittle smile. "Duly noted."

"What is your question?" I asked, bringing the focus back to her reason for showing up in my tent.

"According to Ming, the clown and you were together a lot the last few weeks of his life." She sent a sideways glance toward Bruno, obviously trying to goad a jealous response from him. "Day and night."

Bruno didn't take the bait. He just stood off to the side, listening, his expression interested, but nothing more.

"Clint was a good friend. I won't deny it." I thought of the laughs he inspired while trying to help me out of my lovesick funk. I sent a small smile in Bruno's direction. "He consoled me after Bruno left for his new job, doing his best to cheer me up."

A shadow passed over his face, one corner of his mouth twitching.

"Did Clint mention anything about his past to you?"

I focused on Runash again, weighing my words carefully. "We both agreed from the start that we wouldn't ask questions about anything prior to joining the circus."

"And why is that?"

I shrugged. "There was no need. He was a wereferret and I'm a werecoyote. We didn't want to know anything beyond that for now."

"In the wild, coyotes prey on ferrets."

"In the wild," I shot back, "cougars prey on every single one of us here at the circus."

"Touché." She pointed at the tarot cards I was shuffling. "Let's play with your cards."

"Play what?"

"Fortune-teller."

"What is it you seek to learn?"

"I want to know who killed Clint."

"You think these cards will give you the answer that your hunting skills haven't so far?"

"Isn't this why Bruno was ordered to include you in this case? Your psychic abilities should make things easier for us."

I picked up a hint of disdain and disbelief, almost mocking in her tone. My neck bristled. "Okay, Runash. I'll play along." I shuffled with a purpose. "Time is short. We'll do a simple three-card spread."

She smirked. "Let me guess, past-present-future?"

"No, that's too obscure. I'm thinking more like the status of our current situation, the obstacle in our path, and advice on how to overcome it."

"Isn't that deck a bit smaller than usual?"

I shook my head. "We'll stick to the Major Arcana for this reading."

"What's the Major Arcana?" Bruno asked.

"A suit of twenty-two trump cards taken from the seventy-eight tarot card deck. I use them when I'm looking for more meaningful lessons. You okay with that?" I asked Runash.

"You're the psychic. If you think those cards have the answers, I'm all ears."

I shuffled a little longer, lifting my chin at the challenge in her eyes. She thought I was guilty, I could feel it. What had led her to me, though?

Bruno's initial hostility toward me had made more sense. His had been born of sexual frustration. Runash, though, had only known me for a couple of months. We'd had no run-ins, no sexual chemistry, no reason for her to develop a dislike for me. Yet ever since Clint had died, something lingered behind her eyes when she looked my way. Something guarded, wary. Had Ming been whispering in her ear? From the start, the blogger bitch had rubbed me wrong, her nose digging too deep into my business.

I focused on the cards in my hands, transferring my energy to the deck. When the tarot cards felt keen to be read, I spread them out between us on the table. "Pick three."

She chose quickly, her lack of deliberation speaking of her doubt in the cards and my psychic abilities.

I spread out the three cards between us.

Bruno moved behind me, watching over my shoulder. His closeness bolstered me in the face of Runash's scorn.

"Let's start with our current situation, Clint's murder." I flipped over the first card. It was the Wheel of Fortune card in the reverse position.

Damn. If it had been upright, we would have started out on a happy note. But with it reversed, it stood for bad luck, upheaval, unwelcomed change, a lack of control, and negative external forces.

"What's that mean?" Runash asked.

"I'll explain it when we see the other two. Now on to the obstacle in our path."

The second card was the Tower card in the upright direction. Double damn. Add in some trauma, destruction, chaos, loss, revelations, confusion, violence, pain, tragedy, and natural disasters.

"Let's see what the cards have for advice on how to overcome our problem." I hoped to see the Justice or Strength card when I flipped the final one. If I did, then I might have hope that we'd catch Clint's killer before I ended up in pieces along with him.

The final card was the Magician in the upright position. Willpower, skill, ability, concentration, intellect, and psychic powers.

I rubbed my temples, looking up at Runash. "Have you ever had psychic experiences? Mind-reading? Precognition? Ghost sightings?"

She shook her head. "I live in the here and now, Electra. That's what makes me so good at what I do."

I sensed Bruno bristling behind me at her barbed words.

Reaching behind me, I touched his leg, sending calming vibes his way.

I pointed at the first card, the Wheel of Fortune. "Here's what I read from this—our current situation is shitty at best."

"Are you always this professional with your clients?"

"The Wheel of Fortune card in the reversed position tells a story of bad luck. Clint's death was an unwelcomed change that has caused upheaval amongst all of us here at the circus."

Bruno grunted in agreement.

I touched the second card. "This is the Tower card. Unfortunately, it's in the upright direction, which tells me that the obstacles in our path of discovery about who killed Clint involve trauma and chaos. Our loss of Clint in such a violent way has left us confused where to look. In the process of searching for his killer, there will be some painful revelations as we travel the path to discovery."

Runash rolled her eyes in Bruno's direction. "Surely you're not buying this far-fetched business from your girlfriend?"

Bruno shrugged as an answer, not elaborating further.

"This final card," I continued, "is the Magician in the upright position. It advises using psychic powers along with intellect to find the murderer. Skill and ability will play a role in the search, along with willpower and concentration on the task at hand."

"Well, isn't that convenient." Runash stood, her hands on her hips. "Is this the card spread you used to convince the owner that you needed to be included in the search?" She looked up at Bruno. "You'll have to excuse me if I find it a little too convenient that a psychic is the answer for the problem solving."

I shrugged, leaning back in my chair. "You picked them, Runash," I told her. "I just read them."

"According to the report on Clint's death, you were here in your tent alone at his time of death."

"That's correct."

"How do we know that there wasn't a lovers' tiff between Clint and you?"

I heard Bruno inhale sharply.

"Clint was not my lover. He was a friend."

"Ming mentioned that she saw him leaving your tent at all hours of the night."

"In case you haven't noticed, I don't keep bankers' hours here. None of us do."

Her eyes narrowed. "How do you explain your flier being found on his body?"

On his body? I'd thought it was just somewhere in his tent. How many others had seen that flier and my real name? The urge to flee fast and far on my coyote legs stormed inside of me. Tonight was going to be my last here. I could sense death in the air. My limbs tingled with unspent adrenaline.

"I can't," I told her. "There could be a multitude of reasons for him to have it."

"What do the words 'Nora Mai' mean to you?"

"Nothing."

She scoffed, disbelief clear in her expression.

"Listen," I said. "Whether you believe me or not, here's what I do know." I held up one finger. "First, we still have a murderer on the loose." I raised a second finger. "None of us are safe." Had Runash been doing her job as head of security, Clint would still be alive. I was tempted to mention that as a third fact, but I didn't need her twisting evidence to point at me out of spite.

I heard the sound of voices outside, none that I recognized, and glanced at the clock on my chest of drawers. "They opened the gates. If you'll excuse me, Runash, I need to prepare for visitors. With all of the marketing Ming has been doing, we're sure to have a busy night."

Runash turned to leave. "Oh, one more thing, psychic."

I shuffled the tarot cards back into the larger deck as I waited for her to speak.

"Have you heard of the Gone Were witness protection program?"

I didn't even flinch. "No."

"Interesting." With a nod and a tip of her hat, she left the tent.

I turned to Bruno. "She's going to try to pin this on me. It doesn't take a psychic to figure that out."

"She does seem to have some sort of unchecked hostility toward you."

"Are all of you security folks anti-psychic?"

"I'm not anti-psychic." When I looked at him doubtfully, he shoved his hands in his pockets. "I was angry at you. Now I understand why. I wanted you, but you were out of reach. I turned that frustration into anger and poked at you every chance I could. Any reaction from you was something, better than indifference."

I opened my mouth to apologize for my part in the tension between us, but the sound of someone moving around in my waiting area stopped me. "I have a visitor," I told Bruno.

He nodded. He started toward the exit curtains, but then came back over to me. "Be careful," he whispered. "I'll be around, keeping an eye on you. Tonight when you're done, we're going to look into that crystal ball of yours and see what it has to say about Clint, you, and me."

I frowned. "What are you looking for about us?"

He gave me a quick kiss. "Stick around and I'll show you."

Chapter Seven

I was wrapping up a reading with a leather-clad tuxedo cat shapeshifter who was hitting the road with her punk rock band for a three-month road trip around the southeastern U.S. when Bruno pushed aside the curtains enough to peek in at me.

"So, like, what do you think, Madam?" The girl in the chair opposite me flicked back her long black hair. "Should we skip Atlanta after what the cards showed, or take a chance and play there anyway? I mean, the money is, like, amazing, and I hate to refund all of that cash."

I stood, ready for this long day to be over. "If you aren't worried about getting electrocuted, then go for it."

The girl grinned. "A little juice might be good for the show, you know. Like, really light things up."

Or it could fry someone. "Go with your instincts," I advised. "But you might want to have your roadies put up a lightning rod to be safe."

She gave me a thumbs-up, threw some cash in my jar, and headed out.

Bruno came through the curtains. "I closed you down out front."

"Thanks. I'm wiped."

"You didn't run," he said, sitting down in the seat the punk-rocker had vacated. "I'm surprised."

I'd resisted the urge to flee all night long, telling myself that running was a last resort after all else failed. "Why does that surprise you?" I packed away the cards.

"You're a coyote. Running is one of the things they do best."

"Trust me, I thought about it many times tonight."

"What kept you from following through?"

I looked at him. "Take a guess."

He held out his left hand, palm open.

"What?" I asked, frowning at his hand.

"I want a palm reading."

I hesitated, wondering what game he was playing with me now. "Palm reading isn't very accurate. It's more of a whimsical device."

"It's listed on your sign out front."

"Only because palm reading is not as scary for some as tarot cards and my crystal ball. It's like training wheels for first-time visitors."

He pointed at his open hand. "I'm a first-time visitor. I'd like a palm reading."

I sighed. "Bruno, I'm tired."

"Please, Nora. I promise not to be as skeptical as Runash."

"Fine." I sat down across from him, not yet taking his hand in mine. "You're left-handed."

"Very observant."

I shrugged. "You're my fated mate. There isn't much about you I've missed."

His gaze lowered to my mouth. "There is a lot about you that I plan to discover, but first things first." He made a fist with his left hand. "Is there a problem with me being left-handed?"

"Not a problem, only a different reading than your non-dominant hand." At his lowered brow, I clarified, "If I look at your left hand, I'll be looking for insights into your work and how you present yourself to the world. Is that what you want?"

"What will you see in my right hand?"

"Personal relationships, emotions, and dreams."

His dark eyes held mine as he switched to his other hand. "I already know about my work."

"I thought you were here to find out who killed Clint."

"I'm at the circus to find Clint's killer. I'm in your tent right now because of you."

"I didn't kill Clint."

"I believe you. Now read my palm, please."

I took his warm hand in mine, flattening his fingers. "Hold on, let me get my lamp."

After setting it down between us, I leaned over his palm, starting with the middle line.

"This is your head line. Its length tells me that you tend to think about things for a while before making a decision." I glanced up at him to see if he had any questions about that.

He was staring at me as if I was spread out naked on a magazine page in front of him.

I focused back on his hand. "This is your life line. Look how long it is." I traced it with my nail. "See how it curves around here and ends at the base of your palm? That means you are steady, like a rock. Your friends and others rely on you to stay strong and dependable, especially in difficult times. It makes complete sense with what you do for a living."

"I thought we were talking about my emotions and relationships."

"On this front, the two seem to go hand in hand."

"Do you depend on me?"

"I've wanted to."

"But?"

"But I didn't want you to know the truth about me."

"You think I'm incapable of seeing beyond the crime for the reasoning behind it?" He pointed at his head line. "That right there says I like to mull things over. You should have trusted me sooner, Nora. I wouldn't have left the circus."

"And Clint might still be alive," I finished for him.

"That's not what I was thinking."

"What then?"

"We could have saved months of frustration, pain, and

loneliness—the whole reason Clint was consoling you while I was gone."

"You knowing the truth about who I am doesn't really change anything, though."

He scoffed. "It changes everything, woman."

"I'm still in the Gone Were program, stuck behind a fake identity for the rest of my life. The only thing different now is that I've put you at risk, too."

"I risk my life every day. It's what I do."

"Not for me."

"For you, for Eugene, for everyone here at this circus."

I held his stare for several seconds, then blinked and returned to his palm.

"This is your heart line." I ran my nail along the uppermost horizontal line. You see these three faint Xs near your outer palm? That shows me you've experienced deep betrayal in your life."

"My father," he said, nodding. When I looked up at him, he added, "His leaving before I was born used to eat at me, making me prone to violence. I finally realized that the only way to ease that pain of betrayal was by letting him go." He reached out with his free hand, brushing the back of his fingers down my cheek. "But I held on to my anger, taking it out on anyone of pure lineage."

"I understand."

"I'm sorry, Nora. You didn't deserve my resentment."

"Apology accepted, Bruno." I gave him a small smile. "I'm tough. I can handle a little fire now and then." I returned to his palm. "The shortness of your heart line and the way it curves up here tells me that you are more reserved. You prefer being one-on-one with someone rather than being in a group."

He closed his hand around my finger. When I glanced up, his mouth was open slightly, his chest rising and falling rapidly. "Nora."

"What?"

He took the lamp and set it on the floor. "Come here."

"We need to look for Clint's killer. Remember? That's why you're back."

"I told you, I'm not in your tent right now for Clint, I'm here for you." He stood and pulled me around the table until I was standing in front of him. "Nora," he whispered. He tipped my chin up. "I want to bite you."

"That's a bad idea." While the mating ritual nip was said to be unbelievably pleasurable, I wasn't sure yet that I was going to stick around. If he bit me, it would seal me as his and that could lead to big problems on so many levels.

"You're mine," he challenged.

"Well, yeah, but not officially. I mean, sure we're fated mates, but at this point we can go on with our lives separately, if needed. If you bite me, I'm toast."

"I think you're confused. I wasn't asking for your permission. You're mine and I'm going to bite you."

"Bruno, if I don't want you to bite me, you need to respect my decision."

"I respect a lot of things about you, but on this particular item, I'm not interested in discussing the pros and cons." He took my mouth in a breath-stealing kiss, surprising me into submission.

His hands slid under my tunic, taking up where we had left off when Runash interrupted us earlier. I wanted to resist, at least my head did at first, but then he lifted my tunic over my head and licked me through my camisole, and all thoughts of stopping him floated away.

He lifted me onto the table, the legs creaking under my weight. He grabbed the bottom of my long velvet skirt, lifting it up to my thighs. His hands branded my legs as they trailed north up my calves, over my knees, along my outer thighs. The whole time his tongue worked its magic on me, teasing and flicking, sucking and stroking.

A month's worth of pent-up lust filled me from head to toe,

making me hot, bothered, and wet. The last time we'd done this dance, he'd been drunk and I'd been plagued with guilt for taking advantage of him. This time, he was cold sober. No guilt, just Bruno, hot and hard, pressing against me.

I wrapped my legs around his hips, pulling him closer.

He stared into my eyes as his thumbs slid inside of my underwear, watching me as he stroked, teased, and explored.

I moved my hips, needing more than skimming touches. "Stop teasing me," I gasped as he stroked again.

"I'm going to bite you."

"No."

He pressed, moving his thumb in small circles that made me dizzy with lust.

"You like that?" he asked, still watching me, holding back his kisses.

"You know I do." I reached down and pressed his hand against me, moving with his touch. Pleasure began to build deep in my core, my body tightening.

I pulled away long enough to shove off my underwear, then his hand was back.

"Let me bite you," he said, his finger sliding inside of me, while his thumb continued to rub.

"Bruno, wait," I whispered, my breaths growing shallow, coming faster. My resistance was waning. The thought of his mouth on my skin made me moan in anticipation.

He pulled his hand away and lowered himself to his knees in front of me, licking his way up my inner thigh. His teeth grazed my skin.

"Oh, God," I cried, writhing under his touch, pleasure just out of reach.

"Nora," he whispered, his breath hot on my thigh. "I'm going to bite you."

I shook my head once, but I wanted him to sink his teeth in more than anything else.

He pulled me to the edge of the table, parted my thighs, and then licked me, stroking and delving, making me moan and ache. I leaned back on my hands, opening wider to him, gasping his name, pleading for him not to stop.

I teetered at the edge of pleasure and he pulled back, his lips moving back to my thigh. "Bruno," I breathed, needing him to finish what he'd started.

He rose and stood over me. "Let me bite you." When I hesitated, he added, "I've wanted you since I met you, Nora. You were made for me."

I frowned up at him. "I'm on the run."

"I'll run with you, protect you." He bared his teeth. The shifter reared in him, his canines lengthening, his eyes glowing as his feral side took over. "Let me make you mine, Nora Mai."

The emotion in his voice was my downfall. I was tired of long nights, dreaming about him only to wake up cold and alone. I stretched my leg out along the table, offering myself to him.

He groaned. He bent down and licked my inner thigh before sinking his sharp teeth into my skin.

I tipped my head back, the pain making me cry out at first, but then pleasure rushed over me, tremors of release ripping through my whole body.

Bruno waited for me to come up for air before pulling me against him, his body straining under my hands.

"Bruno," I said, tearing at his clothes. I needed him now!

"Hurry."

I did.

This time there was no drunken fumbling.

No guilt.

No worries about hiding my scent and feelings.

He slid between my thighs and took me with a force that knocked the wind out of me.

I clutched his shoulders as he rocked against me, clinging when I pulsed around him. The tightening of my body seemed to push him over the edge after me. I held him as he groaned and shook with release.

When he finished and looked at me, I saw in his eyes what I'd been waiting for all my life.

"Nora." He raised my hand and kissed my knuckles. "I had no idea."

"Me neither."

"Does it hurt bad?"

I knew he meant the love nip. "It tingles."

He smiled. "You're mine, woman. I'll follow you to the ends of the earth."

I cupped his face, giving him a soft kiss. "How about just following me to my bed for now?"

"I can do better than that." He lifted me, carrying me through the curtains, and lowering me onto my bed. "I'm sorry," he said when he joined me.

"For the bite? Don't be. I wanted you to do it, but I was afraid of what it would mean for you."

"Not for the bite. I wanted to make you mine, plain and simple. I'm sorry for not being here to save Clint."

I hugged him close. "That's not your fault."

His breath was hot on my neck. "Are you on birth control?"

"No, but I'm not ovulating right now."

"Damn."

I chuckled. "But that doesn't mean we can't keep practicing."

He didn't wait for a second offer, moving slower this time, exploring more thoroughly. When I'd had all of the teasing I could take, I pushed him onto his back and leaned over him, sinking my teeth into his shoulder, marking him as my own.

His body tensed for a moment under me, and then he took me by the hips. "There's no going back now, woman," he growled and pulled me down onto him.

"You promise?"

For an answer, he finished what I'd started.

We were still breathing heavily when I heard a sound outside of my tent.

"Electra?" I heard Eugene say quietly through the tent fabric.

Bruno frowned at me. I shrugged, sitting up and looking for my robe. "What do you need, Eugene? If this is about your act tomorrow, you need to come back in the morning when my head is clear."

"It's not the act. I need to talk to you about something I overheard. Can I come into your tent?"

"Sure. Wait for me in my parlor. I'll be out in two shakes."

I kissed Bruno once more before climbing off of him.

Eugene was standing inside the curtains when I joined him, leaving Bruno sitting on the side of my bed.

"What is it?" I asked Eugene. One of his eyes looked redder than the other. "Are you okay?"

He wrung his hands. "I overheard Ming talking to someone in her tent about you."

Me? "What about me?"

"Ming said you aren't who you say you are."

My hands grew clammy. "Did she say who I was?"

"She mentioned the name 'Nora' and told whoever she was talking to that she was going to write a blog about your true identity."

"What?!" I fell into my chair. "Why would she do that?"

Bruno stepped out from my bedchamber, fully dressed again, drawing a curious look from Eugene. "Because Ming is all about promoting the circus, no matter the cost," Bruno answered.

This would draw in the bounty hunters like flies to honey. I needed to run! Now! Far!

Bruno squeezed my shoulder. When I looked up, he shook his head slightly, seemingly reading my mind. It appeared he had some psychic abilities, too.

"Ming said you're a fake," Eugene said.

"That bitch," I muttered.

"Is it true? Are you a fake?"

"No, Eugene. I'm really a psychic. I have not lied to you about your act."

"Then what does she mean?"

I sighed. It didn't matter. I'd have to be gone by morning. "She means I'm not really Madam Electra."

Eugene snorted. "Well, that's no big deal. None of us are really who we say we are here."

I blinked. "We aren't?"

"Well, Bruno's true blue," Eugene said, "but the rest of us all have something to hide. That's why we're here."

"Oh." Maybe I wasn't as good a psychic as I'd thought.

"Ming needs to be stopped," Bruno said, pulling on his boots.

"Where are you going?" I asked.

"To find Ming."

"Not without me," I said, grabbing my slippers.

We parted ways with Eugene when we reached his tent.

Several tent searches later, Bruno and I were still empty handed. We headed back to my place, stopping to pet Jeff, the circus's only rhino, who was enjoying a massage and rubdown by Hank, the gorilla shapeshifter, who treated his pet rhino like royalty.

The sound of a scream made me jerk away from the rhino.

Bruno took off toward the sound of the scream at a sprint. I raced after him into the darkness, but my slippers slid on the dew-covered grass, slowing me down.

The screamer acted as a beacon, drawing a crowd.

"What happened?" I asked Lemon Drop when I reached the group. Or maybe it was Lolli Pop.

"Somebody stabbed Ming."

"What?"

She nodded, her eyes watery. "Ming's dead."

Chapter Eight

An hour later, I paced my tent, waiting to learn who killed Ming.

Finn and Eugene stayed by my side per Bruno's orders, making sure I kept breathing until he returned to my tent. The local law enforcement had been called in to work with Bruno, Runash, and the others on their security team as they analyzed the crime scene.

"Why Ming?" I asked nobody in particular. More important, did it have something to do with what Eugene had overheard about her exposing me? Was someone working undercover here for Gone Were and had been trying to protect me from exposure? Or had Ming pissed off someone else?

"She had a lot of enemies," Finn said, his nose twitching. He spoke in plain English this time. Twice he pulled a joint from his pocket, fingered it, and then stuffed it back into his jacket.

"Eugene, are you sure you didn't see, hear, or smell who she was talking to in her tent?"

"No," the bear of a man said from where he lounged in my parlor room visitor chair. "But I was distracted."

"By what?" Finn asked, his gaze darting around my tent.

"Some of the fire-retardant goop I used had seeped into my right eye during my show. I'd been on my way back from the shower with my eye still burning when I overhead Ming. I only paid attention to the bit I heard about Electra being a fake because she foretells the outcome of my performances each night. As soon as I heard that, I came to Electra's tent to see if Ming was lying or not."

"Well, I doubt you need to worry about tomorrow night's performance," Finn said, pulling out the joint and sticking it into his mouth this time before yanking it out and stuffing it back in his pocket again.

"Why's that?" I asked, settling into my chair.

"Bruno told Kenneth to shut the circus down until they find the killer."

Eugene frowned. "What did Kenneth say to that?"

"He was too busy choking back sobs to say anything," Finn said, hopping over to peek through the curtains into my waiting area. His back leg thumped nervously when he turned back to us. "He just nodded."

"He must have really loved Ming after all," Eugene said. "The shifters over in Clown Alley must be feeling pretty shitty about this. They had a bet going, laying odds on how long until Ming left Kenneth for a bigger fish."

"Maybe that's who killed her." Finn changed feet, thumping with his other one. "A bigger fish."

"Or maybe it's the same person who killed Clint," I said. "Didn't you say that she was stabbed?"

"No, Lemon Drop told you that." Finn's nose twitched in rapid-fire succession. "I heard she was torn to pieces."

My heart hurt for Ming, even though she had been on the verge of destroying my life. Her aspirations had gotten the best of her.

Poor Kenneth. His pug heart wasn't going to fare well with losing her. I wondered if the owner was going to send in a temporary master of ceremonies while Kenneth grieved.

"You don't think they'll shut us down for good, do you?" Eugene asked, using the chair to scratch his back. "I don't mean to sound cold hearted about Ming's death, but I don't want to have to find another job. I just don't fit in well with the normal shifters, and I stick out like Bigfoot among the humans."

"Nah, the owner is too into making money with us," Finn said, sniffing the joint this time before hiding it away. "Ming told me once that we make the most money out of all the different divisions in AC's circus conglomeration. Circuses have grown passé, but freaks are like rock stars."

"We're rock stars?" Eugene said, scratching his chin with his tufted fingers. "I don't feel like a rock star."

I was glad we'd be shut down for at least a couple of days per Bruno's order. That would give me time to make a decision about sticking around or not. The problem now was if I left, Bruno would follow. I didn't doubt for a minute that he meant what he'd said about not leaving my side. No longer was I a one-woman band, and to be fair, I needed to see what Bruno wanted to do before making any decisions.

I heard footsteps coming our way through the grass. I could tell by the cadence that it wasn't Bruno. I shushed Finn and Eugene with my finger to my lips.

The three of us waited to see if we'd have a visitor or not. I heard the tent's outer flap swish. "Madam Electra?" Runash called.

Damn it. I wasn't in the mood to deal with her suspicions tonight.

"In the parlor."

She parted the curtains. "You need to come with me."

"Why?" If she was going to arrest me as a suspect for Ming's death, I was going to call bullshit. Bruno had been with me most of the evening. I couldn't have a better alibi.

"Bruno told me to come get you and bring you to the security tent." She sneered at my parlor table. "You're to bring your crystal ball."

Bruno wanted me to bring Ol' Blue? "I'd rather not." At least not in front of a bunch of strangers.

"He mentioned you might feel that way and told me to tell you it's not a request. It's an order. We need your help with several clues Ming's killer left behind."

I could tell by the way her upper lip curled she wasn't buying my psychic act, even though her superior was.

"No." I stood my ground.

Her eyes narrowed. "What?"

"You heard me. I'm not taking my crystal ball to the security tent. If Bruno needs my help, he can come to me."

For Ol' Blue to work for me, I needed to be somewhere I was comfortable. I'd be squirmy as hell with all of those cops and the rest of Bruno's team watching me work. With my luck, I'd look into my crystal ball and end up somehow seeing myself tied to Ming's murder.

Runash cursed. "Fine. I'll relay the message that you are unwilling to help authorities with Ming's murder investigation."

I shrugged off her guilt trip. "Tell Bruno to come to me and I'll do whatever he needs, but my terms are solid—my tent and him alone."

She started to leave.

"Runash." I stopped her, asking, "Does Bruno have any idea why she was killed? Did it have to do with her blog?"

"Nothing has been determined for certain at this time. If you want to know more, *my* terms are that you need to be in our tent amongst the other security personnel with your crystal ball ASAP."

I lifted my chin. "It's going to be like that, is it?"

"It's definitely going to be like that, *psychic*." She spoke that last word with a wrinkled upper lip and then turned to Finn and Eugene. "I hope you both have solid alibis, boys, because you're on my list of suspects along with Electra." After a final squint in my direction, she left.

"What a bitch," Finn said, sticking the joint in his mouth and lighting up.

"I never have liked her." Eugene crossed his arms. "She told me that eating fire in my bear form was a lame act."

I reached across the table and patted Eugene's arm. "Don't let her get in your head. You sell out almost every night. Fire-eating bears are cool."

"Why does she always have to be so mean?" Eugene asked no one in particular.

Finn blew out a circle of smoke. "She's a werecougar. Have you ever met a nice one?"

Eugene sighed, sounding forlorn. "I wish Clint was here. He would be making us laugh."

We sat for a few minutes in silence, listening to the circus going on outside of my tent. I tried to center myself as a way of calming down. First Clint and now Ming. On top of that, Bruno knew my true identity. Damn. So much had happened in such a short time. Maybe if I could calm down and center my thoughts, I could help Bruno when he returned later.

"Hey, Electra?" Finn said, taking another toke. He squinted through the smoke he blew out, pointing his joint at Ol' Blue. "Why is your ball glowing red? Isn't it usually blue?"

I looked over at Ol' Blue. He was right. There was a weird red glow in the center of the crystal ball.

"Oh no," I whispered.

"Oh no?" Eugene repeated, leaning closer to peer into the ball. "Why 'oh no'? Is a red glow bad?"

"Red symbolizes that there is danger on its way."

"Danger for whom?" Finn asked, his back leg thumping again.

I frowned up from Ol' Blue. "One of us."

Eugene groaned, lowering his big head into his huge mitts. "We're next. I just know it."

"Crikey, mate," Finn said, slipping into his Australian accent. "Maybe it's not a life and death deal, you know? Maybe the danger has to do with your act." Finn tried to sound upbeat, but there was a nervous flutter in his voice.

Eugene groaned even louder and dropped down onto the floor, holding his heart. "I knew it. I'm going to go up like a matchstick the next time I handle fire. That's probably why the ball is showing red. It stands for fire."

I shushed them both and closed my eyes, trying to focus on what might be causing the red glow. My mind traveled back to the southwest desert, turning up to stare at the star-filled night sky. *What is it? What is waiting out here for me to see?*

Something was blocking my mental sight.

"Electra." Finn's voice sounded higher than usual. "It's turning gray now. What does gray mean?"

I opened one eye. Finn was right, the red had turned to gray. It started out light gray and then quickly darkened, swirling like oily smoke.

"Shit," I whispered.

"What is it?" Eugene asked, up on his knees to peer into Ol' Blue with Finn and me.

"Gray symbolizes ill fortune, the darker the worse."

"Shit," Eugene repeated my line. He reached out and tapped the crystal ball with his finger.

I knocked it away, scowling. "Ol' Blue doesn't like that."

"It's gone black," Finn said. "Black is never good. Why is it black? Eugene, you shouldn't have touched it. Now we're all doomed." He took a long drag from the joint, holding in the smoke until his eyes bulged and his ears bent downward.

I slid my fingers over the ball, trying to center myself even more and calm down. Maybe Ol' Blue was seeing my fears, showing them by mistake. A minute later, the ball still showed a black cloud, only the swirling was even more turbulent.

"Fuck," I said. "Black is not good."

"You mean like knifed-to-pieces not good?" Eugene whispered.

"It means really bad stuff is coming."

"I thought you were able to see actual things in the ball," Finn said, blowing smoke over Eugene and me when he talked. "Like a little video showing you the future."

Waving away the smoke, I said, "Sometimes I can see things, but other times it only shows me hints of what is to come, like tonight."

I thought back to when I'd looked into it and saw myself dealing out cards in front of Lolli Pop. Why had it shown me that detail then, but only showed glowing colors now? That made no sense, unless …

Then it hit me. The cards I'd read for Lolli had seemed odd. I thought back to what I'd flipped over for her. First there'd been the jack of hearts, which meant the receiver was continually in someone's thoughts. The second card was an ace of spades, which stood for the death of a friend. The third card had been the ace of diamonds, announcing that there was an important letter to read. The final card was the five of clubs, signifying a meeting soon with an interested party.

What if Ol' Blue hadn't been showing me Lolli's fortune, but rather my own? Maybe I had been continually in the killer's thoughts after the death of Clint. There had been an important letter to read, as in the contract on Clint's head that I'd found in that alarm clock. Finally, I was destined to have a meeting with an interested party. Was that Bruno? Or the killer?

My mind flashed to the rune stones I'd read while visiting Finn. First necessity, shadow, and friction for Clint's death; second was death, dreaming, and magic about someone else questioning the details of Clint's death; third was fertility, true love, and harmony regarding if we'd find Clint's killer.

At the time, I had applied my rune stone readings to Clint's death. But what if I shifted my thoughts and focused the reading on my own situation as a hunted woman?

And what about the tarot cards I'd read for Runash? There was the Wheel of Fortune card in the reversed position telling a story of bad luck—or so I thought. Maybe it was *my* bad luck. The second card was the Tower card in the upright direction, which referred to obstacles in our path of discovery about who killed Clint, as well as trauma, chaos, and confusion. Add to that painful revelations on the path to discovery, and it could fit my own ongoing situation as well as Clint's death.

The final card had been the Magician in the upright position, referring to the use of psychic powers, intellect, skill, and ability. That card could have been referring to me, not Runash.

If this were the case, and the readings had been about me, then …

"Oh my God," I whispered, sitting back in my chair, my heart pounding. "I think I know who the killer is."

"Who?" Finn asked, looking up from the ball.

Before I could answer, I heard the sound of a low growl on the other side of the curtains.

The hair on the back of my neck bristled. My legs twitched, eager to flee the scene.

The curtains swayed, and then Runash stepped through. She held a flare gun in her hand, aiming it at Eugene. "Move one muscle, bear, and I'll light you up."

Finn tried to dart past her, but she snagged one of his ears with a speed that took my breath away. She lifted Finn into the air with ease. Finn's back legs kicked as he struggled to break free, but Runash held tight.

"Hold still, rabbit, or I'll rip out your throat." She crooked her neck and opened her jaws, her sharp canines elongated in a partial shift, her cheeks widening as the cougar showed her true self.

"Finn, do as she says," I cried, holding my hands out to stop her. "What do you want, Runash? If this is about the crystal ball, you can put him down. I'll come with you." Although I was pretty sure I knew what she wanted, now that Ol' Blue had worked its magic.

"This isn't about your psychic bullshit." She held the flare gun steady on Eugene, who had shifted into his grizzly form during the commotion. Stress acted as an automatic flip-switch for him. "I'm not kidding, bear. You will burn if I see you take a single step."

Runash had done what cougars do best—ambush their prey. I should have seen that coming, damn it. I was a coyote, not a rabbit or a bear. It was my fault Eugene and Finn were caught up

in this.

Her amber eyes turned in my direction, a low growl sounding in the back of her throat as she watched me with cat eyes. "You're coming with me, Nora Mai, or I'll kill your friends."

Chapter Nine

My heart pounded in my ears. Either Runash knew my name because of the paper in Clint's pocket or worse, she was the bounty hunter who'd torn poor Clint to pieces. If she shifted, I had no chance. Coyotes rarely escaped cougar attacks in the wild. I would have to keep my head, rely on my cunning and wily skills to stay alive.

On top of that, I couldn't let anything happen to Finn or Eugene. I wouldn't be able to live with myself. But before she followed through on whatever she had planned for me, I needed to know something.

"Did you kill Clint because of the contract on his head? Or did he get in the way of catching me?"

Her lip curled. "That clown was a crook. He'd escaped justice for the last time. Just like you."

"Clint had made a deal with the authorities." At least that was my assumption based off my own dealings with the Gone Were program. "He'd given up his freedom to help stop other criminals. How do you figure that us hiding our true identities, never seeing our families again, and living everyday in fear of being discovered is 'escaping justice'? We're serving time, same as the other criminals."

"You're not behind bars, stuck in a cage, forced to eat rotten meat day after day. You're free to breathe the fresh air, roam unchained, and even mate if you want. That's not serving time, psychic. My job is to make you finish paying for your crimes."

"Tearing Clint to pieces was not *justice*," I said.

"I needed his fingerprint, the rest didn't matter."

Christ. I wasn't dealing with a rational mind here. I was staring down a cold-blooded killer bent on delivering her own twisted, gruesome version of justice. How in the hell was I going to outsmart crazy?

An idea struck. I looked from Eugene, whose round eyes were locked on the flare gun, to Finn. The jackrabbit's gaze darted between Runash and me, his eyes wide with fear.

He focused on me, his nose twitching. "Don't," he said, tugging at Runash's arm with his front rabbit feet.

"Don't what, rabbit?" she asked, clacking her long sharp teeth together next to one of his long ears.

He wasn't talking to her. He'd meant that for me.

But I didn't listen.

I blew out a breath and shapeshifted. My skirt billowed around me, hiding me for a second or two while I slipped around the side of my parlor table.

Runash roared. I peeked up at her face, seeing it start to distort. She was shifting, too. I had to move now!

I raced around her, leaping over Finn, whom she'd thrown to the floor, and sprinted out of my tent into the darkness.

There was only one place I could go and have a chance of escaping her. I needed to find Bruno. With his mixed St. Bernard-coyote breeding, his size was twice mine. He would have a chance at taking on Runash with her sharp claws and deadly bite.

Head down, I ran as fast as I could, weaving through the tents, sniffing the air. I could hear Runash's huffs as she bore down on me, closing the distance between us. I darted through the wildebeests' corral, slinking amid the sleeping herd, leaping over their water trough, trying to slow Runash with my agility. The wildebeests woke up with a start, standing, stomping, and bellowing. Out of the corner of my eye, I saw Runash strike out at one, and then she grunted when another kicked her in the side.

That gave me the moment I needed to sniff the air for Bruno's scent, but all I could pick up was the herd.

Runash roared, making my fur bristle. Adrenaline pumped through me. I dashed out of the corral, aiming for the security tent on the other side of the big top. I'd made it almost halfway there when she leapt through the air and barreled into me. We rolled across the grass, her claws digging into my ribs.

I yipped in pain, struggling to break free and gain my feet again.

But she was bigger, heavier, her claws holding me in place while she pinned me with her body weight, huffing over me. Her lips pulled back, her jaw opening wide.

"Wait!" I said, shifting quickly back to my human form to speak. "I have a deal for you." I didn't give her time to reject it and dove straight in. "If you let me live, we can use my psychic abilities and crystal ball to find others in the Gone Were program."

A drop of saliva dripped off one of her canine teeth onto my neck, but her jaws didn't descend. I had her attention for the moment.

"Think about it. As a team, we could catch so many more who have escaped justice. Hunt them down and make them pay, just like you had to."

She partially shifted, a rarity in the were-world. Her cougar body and claws still held me in place, but her fangs retracted into a human-looking mouth. "Who said I ever had to pay? I'm in it for the money."

"If not you, then who? You are avenging on someone's behalf with each of these deaths, I know it. I can feel it."

Her gaze narrowed, her ears pulling back. "Stay out of my head, psychic. I don't think I like your—"

"Hey, kitty!" Something flew between us.

Runash jerked back and let out a hiss of pain.

A thumping noise sounded next to my ear. I looked over. Finn the jackrabbit tapped his back foot on the ground. In his big buckteeth, he held several whiskers. He spit them on the ground. "You missing a couple of these, kitty cat?"

Runash hissed again, her upper lip pulling back, several whiskers missing on one side. "I'm going to rip you limb from limb like I did that fucking clown."

"I don't think you'll be able to catch me," Finn said. "You're big and slow, and you corner like an elephant."

Runash snarled. "I'll show you who's slow as soon as I finish with—"

A huge paw slammed into Runash with a muffled thud. The big cat flew through the air, landing several feet away and rolling across the grass.

Eugene roared at her, his grizzly body hulking over me, shielding me from the cougar.

"Where's your flare gun now, bitch?" Finn challenged, hopping onto Eugene's back. He peeked over the bear's shoulder. "Electra, get out of here."

I pushed onto my knees, but stayed put. "She'll follow me if I run, and Eugene is too slow to keep up. I need to stay and fight."

"Then fight we will, right, Eugene boy?" Finn hopped off as the bear faced off with Runash, who was back on her feet and circling.

A guttural growl came from Eugene, making the hairs on my neck rise even though he was on my side.

"Stay close to him," Finn told me. "If she can separate you from him, she'll take you. There'll be no bargaining this time, coyote."

Runash had returned fully to her cougar form. She stalked one way and then the other, eyeing us. I had no doubt she was calculating a plan of attack. Fearing for Eugene's life, I tried once more to stop any further bloodshed.

"Runash," I said, still in my human form, naked as the day I was born. "Consider my deal. I can do so much for you. How do you think I ended up in Gone Were in the first place?"

She snarled at me in response, and then she lunged.

Eugene took the brunt of her attack, his jaws wide. She was too fast for his punches, dodging his huge paws, and went for his throat. Finn leapt on her back, sinking his buckteeth into her ear, tearing at it. I shifted back into a coyote, rushing into the fray only to catch a sideswipe from Eugene that sent me tumbling across the grass.

I rolled back up onto my paws, swaying slightly with dizziness. Finn lay on his side next to the two snarling and snapping beasts, his body still.

No! I rushed over to him.

Eugene let out a roar of pain, then Runash went flying again. She landed on her feet and turned to lunge again, her lips pulled back. The scent of blood filled the air.

"Freeze!" a growly voice shouted.

Bruno stood ten yards away at the edge of the clearing, a handgun pointed at the cougar. "Move and I'll shoot, Runash."

Finn groaned at my paws.

Runash's eyes turned to me, narrowing slightly. Then she shot off into the darkness.

"Stay with Nora," Bruno told Eugene and started after Runash, shifting as he ran, leaving his gun and torn clothes on the ground.

Eugene lumbered over as I sniffed at Finn. The bear had a limp in his step. His shoulder was bloody, like Finn's back leg. I shifted back to my human form, lifting Finn in my arms. "We need to get him to a healer quickly."

Eugene sat down, taking a few seconds to return to his human form, too. "As soon as Bruno returns, I'll grab some clothes and take Finn to a local veterinarian."

I nodded. "He'll heal quicker since he's in his rabbit form." Shapeshifters healed best when in their animal form. It was one of the blessings that came with the risk of fleas and the need to buy new clothes frequently.

A roar came from somewhere in the trees, followed by a series of gruff barks and goosebump-inducing growls.

I frowned into the darkness, my heart pounding. "Bruno?"

Then there was silence.

I stood slowly, Finn still in my arms, and stared toward the trees, holding my breath.

"Breathe, Electra," Eugene said, standing next to me. He pulled me partially behind him, shielding Finn and me.

The bushes rustled and trembled.

Bruno walked out, a human again—a naked one at that, like Eugene and me, but among shifters bare flesh or fur rarely concerned us. He was holding the cougar by the scruff of her neck. Runash hung limp. As he drew closer, I could see the blood on his thigh and the right side of his chest.

"Give me Finn," Eugene said, taking the jackrabbit from me. "I'll be back when he's been fixed up." He took off.

Bruno threw Runash down on the ground next to his torn clothes, then grabbed what was left of his shirt and wrapped it around me. The shredded cotton hung to my trembling knees.

He grabbed the lapels and pulled me close, kissing my forehead. His warmth stilled my shivering.

"Are you okay?" he asked huskily.

I looked over at where Runash was slowly reverting to her human form, her eyes wide and sightless as she stared up toward the stars.

"I am now." I touched his cheek, wiping away a streak of blood. "What about you?"

"It's going to take some kisses and a lot of licking on your part," he said with a grin. "But I'll be okay by morning."

Chuckling, I leaned my forehead against his chest. "Now what?"

"Now I find some clothes. It's fucking cold out here, and unlike Eugene I'm not thrilled about showing off my fishing tackle to the rest of the circus."

I smiled up at him. "Well, it *is* the freakshow ..."

He smacked my bare backside. "Damned cheeky broad." He tugged me toward my tent.

Chapter Ten

Two nights later …

I packed up my tarot cards in my chest of drawers and took down several of the gauzy veils I used to decorate my tent, folding them as my thoughts drifted to the crystal ball on my parlor table.

In the last two days, Ol' Blue hadn't told me anything I hadn't already figured out, but Bruno had a few crumbs to share that were news to me.

It turned out that Runash had been playing big, bad bounty hunter for years. She had over fifty kills credited to her in the form of payment per hide. Unofficially, Clint's death could be added to that total, but she'd never turned in his finger, which was her preferred choice of proof—a fingerprint of the victim. Bruno found Clint's finger in a sealed plastic bag hidden among Runash's belongings when they searched her tent the night of Ming's death.

Poor Ming had been another of Runash's victims. According to Kenneth, Ming had broken up with him before the show that night because she'd found out some new key information that was supposedly going to boost her career high enough that she didn't need the circus anymore … or Kenneth. That "information" was about me, my fake death, and the crimes attached to my name. Kenneth didn't know this, but Bruno did. He went through Ming's belongings first thing in the morning yesterday, piecing more of the puzzle together.

Ming must have told Runash of her plans, or somehow let it leak, because Ming was torn to shreds much like Clint. Why she felt the need to blab to Runash, Bruno didn't know. He suspected she wanted help catching me in case I tried to run, maybe even a pseudo arrest, and alerted Runash. That had been Ming's fatal mistake. Runash wouldn't have wanted anyone else to know about me, because she was a lone hunter and I was easy prey if nobody else came sniffing around for me.

I tucked away the veils, stuffing them in the drawer next to my rune stones. Clint's clock sat on the corner of my parlor table, the hands frozen in time. I picked it up, a small smile coming to my lips at the memory of his crazy clown laugh as he'd roll around the circus in those big yellow shoes on his metal roller skates. There would never be another clown like him.

I buried his clock under my veils so they'd cushion it. If only I could have figured out Runash's secrets before she ambushed Clint that night in his tent. The poor wereferret didn't have a chance.

I was taking down the curtain that divided my parlor from the waiting room when Lolli Pop strolled inside my tent. "Hey, Lolli."

"I'm Lemon."

I chuckled. "Sorry. One of these days maybe I'll get you two straight. What's going on?"

"I just wanted to tell you that we're planning on having a little memorial for Ming on the train tomorrow morning."

"Thanks. I'll be there."

"Good. We were kind of hoping you would lead it."

"Me? What about Kenneth?"

"He's too heartbroken. We all thought you would be more comforting. You always find a way to make us feel better."

I nodded. "Well, I won't bring any of the tricks of my trade to work my magic," I said with a wink. "But I think I can come up with a few things that will help."

"Thanks. I have to run. I need to go help Lolli load all of our boxes and rings."

"Oh, Lemon," I said, stopping her. "What's going on with Tom and you and your sister?"

"We broke up with him."

"Both of you?"

She nodded. "We agreed that no man was worth fighting over. Family trumps sex, even if he was amazing with the way he—"

"That's enough," I said, grimacing. Hearing about cat sex was not my thing. I couldn't get past the idea of a barbed penis.

She giggled. "I just remembered, Finn wanted me to tell you that he has some brownies he made to thank you." She glanced over her shoulder and then lowered her voice. "He scored some peyote out in Tinkerville and thought you needed something to help you chill."

I already had something that helped me chill—Bruno. That man in my bed did wonders for my stress level. Not to mention that he'd managed to locate my parents and make sure they were safe and doing well. He'd also scored their address, which I'd hidden away for now. Contacting them might not be wise, seeing as how it could put their lives at risk. But I really missed them …

I smiled at Lemon. "How's Finn doing?"

"He's totally healed. That vet in town is freaking amazing. She had him all fixed up in no time. Eugene, too."

I smiled. Eugene had stopped by earlier. Not only had the veterinarian mended Eugene's injuries, but she'd also inspired his self-confidence somehow. He hadn't needed me to do a reading for him before his last show here in Tinkerville earlier this evening. He claimed fire was now his friend.

"Too bad Kenneth couldn't go to her to have his broken heart stitched," I said. The poor man was a sniffling, watery werepug mess with Ming gone.

"He told Lolli he's taking a break from the circus," Lemon Drop said.

"Who's going to be our ringmaster?"

"My adopted uncles."

"Well, that should be entertaining." The monkey brothers would certainly bring new life to the show.

"With Bruno back as head of security, it feels like we're one big happy family again," Lemon Drop said, but then frowned. "Except for Clint and Ming, of course."

I patted her on the shoulder. "The pain will ease with time. Besides, Clint would hate to see you frowning."

She smiled. "You're right. I'd better go. I'll talk to you later." She zipped away, leaving me to my packing.

I'd decided to stay with the circus, even though my cover was partially blown. Bruno, Finn, and Eugene all agreed to keep quiet. Publicly, they'd continue calling me Electra, and help me lay low until Runash's deeds were no longer exciting news.

I had a family now, plus a mate. Running no longer appealed to my coyote blood.

An hour later, everything but my bed and parlor chair had been packed and prepped to load on the train when Bruno came into the parlor and sat down in the chair.

He yawned. "I'd forgotten how busy it is the night before we leave."

"What's the name of the next town?"

"Tippytoe, Louisiana." He smirked. "According to Finn, there is a gang of weremuskrats there that I need to be ready to round up. They like to spray paint our signs and scare the lady flamingos."

"Sounds like you're going to be busy."

He eyed my camisole and matching silky shorts. "Not that busy. Come here."

"What's the magic word?"

"Come here and let me read your palm, beautiful."

Grinning, I walked over and sat on his lap. He took my hand in his, holding it out, tracing the lines as he looked down at it.

"According to this heart line here, there's going to be a lot of sex in your future."

"That's my dominant hand. Are you saying I'll be having sex while working?"

He lifted my palm to his lips. "That depends on your definition of working."

"Telling fortunes to paying clients?"

"I'm talking about your other job."

"What job is that?"

"Attending to your fated mate's many needs."

"My fated mate has turned out to be very needy. I'm going to have to start charging for all of the attending he requires."

He smiled against my lips. "Add it to my bill, Nora Mai." He kissed me slowly, soothing away the last of my stress for the evening. Then he stood, carrying me into the bedroom. "Now, attend me, woman."

My laughter turned to moans moments later while he worked his unique brand of magic on me.

The End ... for now

Look for more laugh-filled mysteries with Nora, Bruno, and the rest of the traveling freakshow gang in *A Bunch of Monkey Malarkey* (the 2nd installment in the AC Silly Circus Mystery Series) in print, ebook and audio.

About the Author

Ann Charles is a USA Today bestselling author who writes award-winning mysteries that are splashed with humor, romance, paranormal, and whatever else she feels like throwing into the mix. When she is not dabbling in fiction, arm-wrestling with her children, attempting to seduce her husband, or arguing with her sassy cat, she is daydreaming of lounging poolside at a fancy resort with a blended margarita in one hand and a great book in the other.

Facebook (Personal Page):
http://www.facebook.com/ann.charles.author

Facebook (Author Page):
http://www.facebook.com/pages/Ann-Charles/37302789804?ref=share

Twitter (as Ann W. Charles):
http://twitter.com/AnnWCharles

Ann Charles Website:
http://www.anncharles.com

More Books by Ann

Books in the Deadwood Mystery Series

WINNER of the 2010 Daphne du Maurier Award for Excellence in Mystery/Suspense

WINNER of the 2011 Romance Writers of America® Golden Heart Award for Best Novel with Strong Romantic Elements

Welcome to Deadwood—the Ann Charles version. The world I have created is a blend of present day and past, of fiction and non-fiction. What's real and what isn't is for you to determine as the series develops, the characters evolve, and I write the stories line by line. I will tell you one thing about the series—it's going to run on for quite a while, and Violet Parker will have to hang on and persevere through the crazy adventures I have planned for her. Poor, poor Violet. It's a good thing she has a lot of gumption to keep her going!

Short Stories from Ann's
Deadwood Mystery Series

The Deadwood Shorts collection includes short stories featuring the characters of the Deadwood Mystery series. Each tale not only explains more of Violet's history, but also gives a little history of the other characters you know and love from the series. Rather than filling the main novels in the series with these short side stories, I've put them into a growing Deadwood Shorts collection for more reading fun.

The Jackrabbit Junction Mystery Series

Bestseller in Women Sleuth Mystery and Romantic Suspense

Welcome to the Dancing Winnebagos RV Park. Down here in Jackrabbit Junction, Arizona, Claire Morgan and her rabble-rousing sisters are really good at getting into trouble—BIG trouble (the land your butt in jail kind of trouble). This rowdy, laugh-aloud mystery series is packed with action, suspense, adventure, and relationship snafus. Full of colorful characters and twisted up plots, the stories of the Morgan sisters will keep you wondering what kind of a screwball mess they are going to land in next.

The Dig Site Mystery Series

Welcome to the jungle—the steamy Maya jungle that is, filled with ancient ruins, deadly secrets, and quirky characters. Quint Parker, renowned photojournalist (and lousy amateur detective), is in for a whirlwind of adventure and suspense as he and archaeologist Dr. Angélica García get tangled up in mysteries from the past and present in exotic dig sites. Loaded with action and laughs, along with all sorts of steamy heat, these two will keep you sweating along with them as they do their best to make it out of the jungle alive in every book.

The Goldwash Mystery Series

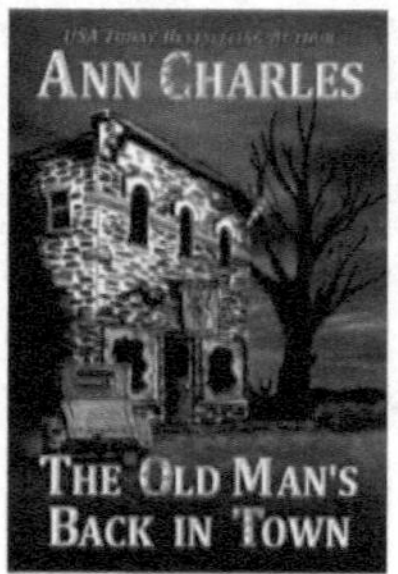

A sizzling, suspenseful SHORT STORY wrapped in a puzzling mystery that will leave you hungry for more.

It's "Groundhog Day" meets the modern day Old West!

In the lonely mining ghost town of Goldwash, Nevada, Christmas has come early. Unfortunately, the local bar owner must be on this year's naughty list, because Santa brought her something even worse than a piece of coal on this dark, cold winter night—her old man.

www.ingramcontent.com/pod-product-compliance
Lightning Source LLC
Chambersburg PA
CBHW032050180726
48284CB00004B/1266